Nicholas E

Bank

BANK

Also by Nicholas E Watkins

Tanker

Dealer

Oligarch

Steel

Hack

About the Author

Nicholas Watkins lives on the Coast with his wife and has four children He is a retired Accountant and has a Degree in Economics. He worked in the City of London for many years.

BANK

Copyright © Nicholas E Watkins 2017

The right of Nicholas E Watkins to be identified as the Author of the Work has been asserted by him in accordance with the Copyright, Designs and patent Act 1988.

All rights reserved. No part of this publication my be reproduced, stored in a retrieval system, or transmitted, in any form or by any means without the prior written permission of the publisher, nor may be otherwise circulated in any form of binding or cover other than that in which it is published and without a similar condition being imposed on the subsequent purchaser.

All characters in this publication are fictional and any resemblance to real persons living or dead is purely coincidental.

Chapter 1

The Sun beat down on the three man, scorching their skin and evaporating the moisture from their bodies. The ropes binding them cut deeply into their wrists and ankles. They lay on their backs facing the sky, the Sun blinding them and blistering the skin on their faces. They had been in the back of the flat bed truck for three hours as it bounced over the arid rocky terrain driving deeper into the Mexican countryside.

The two men upfront, in comfort in the air conditioned cab, were listening to the music on the radio. "Stop I need a leak," said the passenger.

The driver pulled over and they both stepped from the truck, stretching their legs. The passenger climbed up onto the back of the truck. He stood over the three captives in the rear. "Are you thirsty my friends?"

There was no response. They were barely conscious, with lips cracked and large blisters on their foreheads and noses as their skin burnt in the Sun. He unzipped his trousers. Looking at the driver for approval, who laughed at the sight, he began to urinate on the captives. "Drink my friends."

He rotated his body from side to side ensuring that each of the unfortunates received their fair share. They hardly had the strength to move their heads as the stream of yellow urine splashed down on them. They were almost grateful. The piss cooled as it evaporated in the mid day Sun. With a final shake he climbed down from the rear of the truck. Getting back into the cab they continued their journey along the rough track, kicking up a dust cloud as they drove. The dust stuck and clung to their damp bodies in the back, irritating their eyes and skin further as the Sun continued to beat down.

The hut stood on its own with pink mud plastered walls and faded paint peeling wooden shuttered windows. It was the only shade for miles around. There was a well to the front, which had run dry years before, making any form of farming untenable. Abandoned, it had become a useful hideout from prying eyes for the Drug Cartel these men worked for. To one side of the hut was stacked a pile of old truck tyres.

The extreme poverty in Mexico made the rise of the drug industry easy. It was now the direct employer of half a million Mexicans. Mexico was the gateway to the United States for hash and cocaine from Latin American. It was truly big business, with another four million people indirectly dependent on the trade for their livelihoods. With such big stakes the various Drug Cartels would go to extreme lengths to preserve their share of the business. One such Cartel was headed by Jesus Rojas and it was for him that these men worked.

The three men were dragged from the truck into the darkened interior of the adobe hut. They were left bound on the compacted mud floor, while their captors opened the shutters letting in shafts of sunlight illuminating the single room. "Do not die my friends. At least do not die before the boss arrives," said the driver as he poured water into each of the men's mouths in turn. Their captors lit cigarettes and settled down to wait.

Rojas sat on the back seat of the limo. Alongside him was his seventeen year old companion, a stunning beauty with long black hair, slim long legs and prominent small breasts. She wore very little, an almost transparent white dress through which, when the light shone, her dark nipples were visible. She never wore panties. She loved the feel of eyes on her body. She was an exhibitionist and Rojas loved it that way. The sight of his men furtively looking at her body aroused him and he encouraged her to indulge herself to the extreme in her tendencies.

Rojas was in his mid fifties and did as he pleased. He had risen in the drugs world through self determination and a passion for violence. He liked killing and he liked to be hands on. He had taken time out to come to the isolated hut in the middle of nowhere to personally take charge of these men's punishment.

The three men were his employees and had worked for him, transporting hash across the border to the US. They had felt they were worth more than the money Rojas paid them. They had wanted to branch out on their own and start their own little business empire. Rojas wondered why these people thought he was stupid. Surely they must realise he did not stay number one by letting every peasant who wanted to just walk in and steal his business. He reasoned that it was time to send a message to all those thinking of competing against him.

"Nobody fucks with me and gets away it," he thought. "Not even the Yankees." On the pull down table, in the back on the limousine, he had a large bowl of cocaine which his companion had been helping herself to on their long drive. He pulled her dress down exposing one breast fully. He could see the driver looking at her tits in the rear view mirror. He positioned her so he could get a better view. Taking a small spoon he laid a line across the top of her breast and inhaled. He felt the rush of euphoria and power. He knew at that moment he was invincible. She made no attempt to cover her breast and left it exposed for the driver to admire. Smiling and aroused she pulled her dress up. revealing her dark pubic hair. She gently masturbated. The mix of cocaine and the anticipation of the violence to come stirred her lust and aroused her.

"No body fucks with Jesus Rojas," he repeated. He thought of how the CIA man had died only two weeks before. He had been down in Mexico working with Drug Enforcement as part of America's war on drugs. He had made a nuisance of himself. This had annoyed Rojas. So he sent a message to the CIA in the form of his decapitated head.

The car pulled up at the hut. A second car pulled in behind them and discharged four men armed with light machine guns. His bodyguard did a sweep checking in and around the hut before opening the door to his heavily armoured car. His companion made sure that the guard, who opened the door on her side, got a glimpse of her breast and pubic region before pulling her dress up and letting the skirt fall as she stepped from the limo.

As Rojas's eyes became accustomed to the darkened interior, he could see the three bound unfortunates sitting in the centre of the room. The smell of shit filled the air and it was clear that the younger of the bound men, no older than Rojas' female companion, had defecated in fear. "You should shit yourselves my friends. I would shit myself if I were caught stealing from Jesus Rojas."

Addressing his men he said, "Get them outside, it stinks in here."

The bodyguards had moved the truck tyres about two hundred metres from the hut and arranged them in a neat line about fives metres apart. The captives were pulled, still bound from the building. They blinked in the full Sunlight. The young boy was crying and pleading. The older men just looked grim faced at the row of tyres. They knew that Rojas would show no mercy and begging was a waste of time. They knew his reputation as a sadist. They also knew how debauched and corrupt the young whore, who he liked to exhibit, was. So young, but so perverted, her every fantasy indulged by Rojas.

The men still tied were lifted one by one into the centre of the stacked tyres, their heads and shoulders poked from the top. A can of gasoline was taken from the boot of the second vehicle and part of its contents was poured liberally over each tyre and its captive filling. Necklacing was the name they penned for putting the victim in a tyre, filling it with petrol and setting it on fire. The young girl, wide eyed was becoming increasingly sexually aroused as the gasoline was poured over the first victim, the next and then the next. She reached between her legs. Pulling her skirt up she began to rub herself. In her state of cocaine induced heightened sexual arousal, she was indifferent to the men looking at her.

A piece of cloth was round tightly around a charred stick that had clearly been used many times before as a torch. It was dipped in gasoline and lit. The horror in the eyes of the three victims was clearly visible. They knew what their fate was to be. The remains of previous burnt tyres were scatted around them, dispelling any doubts.

Rojas's bodyguards and his driver left in the second car. "Come back in an hour," he said. The girl, impatient, pulled her dress off without waiting for the departure of the truck that had delivered the three prisoners for execution. Eagerly she picked up the burning brand and set fire to the first capture. She rubbed her cunt and watched him scream and slowly roast. She was in a frenzy of lust and drug induced euphoria.

Rojas stripped naked, his penis fully aroused as he watched her set fire to the second and third piles of rubber and flesh. He lay on his back with his feet pointing towards the burning and screaming men. She thrust down hard onto his erect penis, her facing towards his head and she, facing the screaming, burning men. She fucked as she watched the men roast in the flames.

The distant scene unfolded in the scope of the sniper's rifle. He saw the look of ecstasy on her young face as she fucked. He pulled the trigger and a red dot appeared on her forehead. She slumped, toppling forward onto the knees of Rojas. He without realising she was dead carried on thrusting.

Her lack of response finally and slowly entered Rojas's consciousness. He pushed himself upright. She slid to the side. He now saw she was dead but he hardly had time to process this information before he too died from the sniper bullet, fired from nearly half a mile away, entering through his left eye and exploding his brain.

The assassin lay the riffle down on the ground beside him. Abandoning it, he started the engine of the motorbike and drove across the rough terrain towards the two dead bodies. He reached them in a matter of minutes. He inspected Rojas's body, ensuring he was dead. He could hear the screams of the young boy burning. He pulled out a pistol and shot him, in the head, ending his suffering.

He looked down on the two intertwined bodies and reached into his pocket. He pulled out two white feathers and placed one on each of them. He started his bike and drove off. He had done his job and would soon be on a plane heading for the next contract killing.

There was a knock on the Director's office door at CIA headquarters in Langley. The door opened and the deputy director walked in. "Just thought I would let you know that Jesus Rojas seems to have met an unfortunate death."

"It would seem you can't fuck with the CIA and get away with it after all," said the Director.

Chapter 2

Mrs Routledge and her daughter Jacqueline, were out shopping on Muswell Hill Broadway in North London. It was a Saturday and the shops were crowded. She had driven over from the family home in Pinner and had stayed with her daughter the previous evening, so that they could get an early start.

"Tim seems to get on so well with Daniel." They had taken a break and were sitting in Starbucks. Mrs Routledge had moaned about the price of the coffee as usual.

"They get on like a house on fire. Daniel is so happy to be like the other boys and loves it when Tim drops him at school," said Jackie. She had meet Tim Burr after she had gone out for a drink with work colleagues. Her drink had been spiked by a couple of louts who had been intent on ending the evening with a bit of non consensual sex. Tim had intervened and taken her home. They subsequently met up and the relationship had quickly grown from there.

"Does he ever see Jimmy?" asked Mrs. Routledge. James Milligan was Daniel's Father. Daniel was nine years old and his Father had not seen him for years. They had been officially divorced for two years. Jackie had now changed back to her maiden name, Routledge, to purge herself of the taint of her husband. Jimmy had been twelve years older than her. To her aged twenty two, he had seemed handsome, sophisticated and more grown up than the students with whom she had been going out with up to then. He was always well groomed and looked successful. He told her that he had been married before but his wife had cheated on him and left him for another. He said he had no children. She believed him. Her Father did not. He did some checking and it turned out that Jimmy had two daughters and his wife had a restraining order granted against him. Of course being young Jackie knew better and believed Jimmy.

They got married and he, having nowhere to live and having no means of supporting himself, had moved in with her and her parents. They were happy and despite her Father's misgivings things seemed to go alright. Jackie spent the next three years qualifying as a Chartered Accountant and they eventually moved out of her parent's home.

As her earnings increased they bought a flat with the help of a deposit provided by her parents. Then things changed. It began small. There would be criticism as to the way she dressed, then her time of getting home or where she had been. The signs were there but she ignored them and blamed herself and tried to please him. She fell pregnant with Daniel and by then, Jimmy was going out drinking. He started to come home drunk and would lose his temper when the food she made was not to his liking. That was the first time he hit her. She was seven months pregnant

He was so sorry the next day and bought her flowers. He promised that it would never happen again. It did of course, regularly. She tried her hardest to please him but she just couldn't get it right. She believed that it was her fault and she knew that after Daniel was born, her husband was not getting the attention he deserved

The rapes began two weeks after the birth. She was not ready for sex yet but Jimmy came back drunk, as usual and called her a bitch and raped her anyway. She knew things were not right but she was ashamed. She hid or thought she hid the bruising from her work colleagues and pretended all was normal. The restrictions grew and her freedom and her will were gradually being sapped. She had to keep her eyes down when they took Daniel out. If Jimmy thought he saw her looking in the direction of another man, that was cause for a beating. She would be accused of being a whore, a tart and a slag, if she even spoke to the postman.

It was Daniel's fifth birthday party and his friends from school and their Mums were there. Jimmy had promised to be there, but he found he had urgent business in the pub with his drinking mates. He arrived back at about half seven very drunk and wanted sex. She was bathing Daniel prior to putting him to bed. Jimmy came in the bathroom furious that she had not stripped and gone into the bedroom. Daniel was still in the bath. Jimmy punched her in the face and pushed his sons head under the bath water. "If he takes up so much time I'll drown the little fuck," he screamed at her.

She fought like only a Mother can for her child. Eventfully, she had her son and got him to his bedroom and settled him. She was bruised and battered and knew that this was the end. She had to endure another beating as he raped her and blamed her for his inability to ejaculate. She sucked his penis until her lips were swollen. It was her fault he could not come and not the all-day drinking binge and the vast amount of whisky he had consumed.

With Jimmy passed out naked on his back, snoring and stinking of whisky, she eventually managed to muster the courage to leave. She turned up on her parent's doorstep, with two carrier bags containing her and Daniels clothes, Daniel and their cat.

Jimmy did not give up easily and over the following months he did everything from threats to faking a suicide attempt and threatening to kill her in order to get her to come back. She was done with him. The attack on Daniel was the key that opened her eyes to the nasty, wife beating bully he was.

"No, he has never had an interest in him," said Jackie in reply to her Mother's question as to if, Daniel had any contact with his Father.

Her romance with Tim could only be considered whirlwind in anybody's book. Dinner, passionate love making, days out with Daniel, passionate love making, evenings out together, passionate lovemaking, dinner with friends and passionate lovemaking. They knew they were in love from the start. It had been natural and easy. He had made the World seem brighter. Tim and Daniel had taken to each other and were now inseparable.

The marriage proposal and ring came within a month and they had a slot at the Registry Office in a week. A Wednesday, granted not the best day, but still the best day for her and Tim. There was even a small advantage to having changed her name back to Routledge, to wipe clean her connection to Jimmy. She would now, at least be Mrs Burr, which although not a great deal of improvement as names go, it was nevertheless an improvement. "Come on, hurry up." said her Mum, "We have to be at the wedding dress shop in ten minutes."

Chapter 3

Enrique Rojas had just become one of the most powerful and wealthiest men in Mexico. In his thirties, short and with pock marked skin he did not look the epitome of success. He looked more suited, in appearance, to running a seedy cantina, or dealing drugs on the street corner. His clothes and jewellery betrayed his wealthy background. Rolex, Gucci and Armani were his staple. Not a statement of taste, but merely a reflection of his bank balance. In truth, he had dealt drugs on street corners and his Mother had worked cleaning and any other job that put food on the family table. His Father set the standard of criminality for him to emulate from an early age.

They had lived in the slums of Mexico City, he, his brother and his parents. One room, no toilet and a stand pipe to wash. As a small child, he could remember his Father coming home in the early hours, often covered in blood. Usually his Father bore the marks of having been in a fight, sometimes a knife wound, other times bruising to his face and knuckles. Then his Father had been shot. He remembered his Mother being frantic, screaming, crying and fighting to stop the flow of blood. She had retreated to the corner of the room, sitting on the floor. She had wrapped her arms around him and his brother and rocked back and forth tears rolling down her cheeks. She and his Father were in their mid twenties and he was ten and his brother eight. He was so frightened, he hardly dared breathe for fear of even that small movement in the air, might cause his Father to leave them.

The traffic was appalling as usual and he looked at the chaotic scenes through the window of the heavily armoured Mercedes. Two men sat in the front, his bodyguards. Things had certainly changed from that night when he thought his Father would die. Now he lived in a luxury villa, had a fleet of cars, a yacht and a private jet was available to him. He thought back to that fateful night as the car made its way into the countryside. He would have plenty of time to reminisce. The journey would be over in three hours.

Alone with his thoughts his mind took him back to that night which he now realised had been the turning point in their lives. His Father had been no more than a petty criminal on the fringes of the drug trade. He ran messages, did a bit of debt collecting and acted as a sometime muscle for hire. Enrique knew his Father to have a violent temper and when enraged had no fear. He and his brother had often experienced his Father's wrath and they feared him more than they loved him. That night, holding his Mother and brother, watching him slowly bleeding out, he had feared the impending loss and experienced some feelings of love.

He could see tears in his brother's eyes and understood the confusion he was experiencing. They were used to their Mother patching their Father up after his various violent escapades, but this was different. He and his brother could sense it. Their Father, Jesus was dying. He lay, on the now blood stained, bed where he and his wife slept. The two boys slept in the far corner. The mattress, which during the day was lent against the wall, would be laid flat at night for them to sleep on. A curtain would be pulled around them to divide them from their parents and offered them a small amount of privacy. Enrique remembered staring at the single light hanging in the middle of the room. He stared at it until his eyes were dazzled and spots began to appear. By fixing on the light, the sound of his Father's moans seemed more distant and less penetrating.

There was a noise as a group of men entered the room. It startled his Mother and the two boys. Enrique could not make out what was happening at first. He needed to adjust his eyes to see clearly. He heard his Mother begin to scream. Three men had entered. They were immaculately dressed and one carried a doctor's bag. "Shut up you stupid bitch," one said. "We are here to help him not hurt him."

The doctor lent over Jesus and pulled his hands from the blood soaked rag his wife had tried to stem the flow of blood with. Jesus let out a yell of anguish as the doctor examined the wound. "It is bad. We need to get him to hospital. Help me." Just like that, the room was silent his Father gone. It had taken three days for his Mother to locate him. She found him in a private clinic. They had walked for miles and caught several buses to get there. He and his bother were exhausted by the time they entered the hospital bedroom. Jesus was unconscious and tubes and wires were connected to all types of medical monitoring equipment.

"We could live here," said Enrique's brother, "it has such a nice bed and is so clean and bright." They laughed and felt happy for the first time in days. Jesus would live.

The car was speeding along the highway further into the county and the light was beginning to fade. The sky was deep lavender with a golden band of yellow and red on the horizon. The land seemed to float in the distant haze as the Sun disappeared. Now Jesus was dead and his son was on his way to see his Father for the last time.

After his Father came back from hospital things changed rapidly. They moved to a bright spacious apartment. They had cars, holidays and he and his brother attended a good school. Jesus, in that single night, had changed the course of all their lives. He liked to refer to it as that magic bullet that made him rich.

He had not gone out that night expecting anything to be different. He had been hanging around in the cantina hoping to pick up some work for the drug cartel. He was drinking cheap whiskey and probably had too much. Whisky always made him feel braver and more aggressive.

BANK

The head of the drug cartel rarely consorted with the rank and file, but that night he had appeared. He had scheduled a meeting with a rival drug lord to sort out a turf war and attempt to cut back on the murder rate. The boss and his guards had taken up seats at a table facing the door. Then it had all happened in a split second. One of the guards rose to his feet and began shooting into the room. They were all taken by surprise and several died before they moved. They doors flew open and men firing automatic weapons entered. By now, the occupants had their guns out and were firing back. Jesus was only yards from the boss and saw one of his body guards draw his gun and turn, aiming to shoot his boss in the head.

Jesus did not know why he had not dived for the ground for cover, but he hadn't. Not thinking, he threw his glass at the body guard as it, miraculously, hit him in the face. The gun went off. The assassin's bullet flew harmlessly into the ceiling. Jesus had his knife in hand and with one swift movement sliced deep into the assassin's throat, preventing him from firing a second time. He pulled the drug lord clear of the table and half dragged him to the rear of the cantina. He, by now recovering his wits, pulled his gun and began firing back at the attackers. That was when the bullet hit Jesus and he fell to the floor. He staggered from the building and made his way home to die.

Jesus' boss survived the attack unscathed and in gratitude paid for the doctor and hospital treatment. While Jesus lay recovering in hospital, his boss embarked on the most bloody drug war in years. People died daily and bodies were piling up in the street. He emerged the winner and the most powerful drug lord in Mexico. On leaving hospital Jesus became his most trusted lieutenant.

Jesus killed his boss six years later in a brutal coup, where twenty six others died. He now became the most powerful and richest drug baron in Mexico. At the time of the coup, Enrique and his brother worked for the Cartel. His Father became all powerful, but he lost a son and Enrique lost a brother in the takeover. Enrique was alone now that his Father was dead. His Mother had died at the age of forty from breast cancer.

Finally, he reached the mud hut, miles from anywhere. Enrique stepped from the limo. Three cars pulled up behind him and fifteen of his men stepped out, all carrying Uzi machine guns. He had not been sure what to expect, but he was not going to be caught unprepared. He saw the remains of three smouldering tyres containing the charred and blackened bodies encased in them. His Father was just supposed to be carrying out a routine execution of three nobodies who had tried to steal from the Cartel. Enrique knew that his Father had, as he got older, enjoyed getting hands on in these matters, but he could not understand how things had gone so badly wrong.

Enrique walked forward and the men surrounding his Father's body stepped aside. His Father was on his back with a neat bullet hole in the centre of his body. A naked girl was slumped forward, still sitting on his penis. She too had a bullet hole in her head. Two white feathers were on the bodies.

"Get that whore off him and cover him up." Riga mortis had set in and they struggled to separate them. There were cracking noises as they were eventually parted. "What happened?"

One of Jesus' bodyguards came forward. "We drove him here and as you can see he ordered us to torch the three scumbags. While she watched them burn she got horny and wanted to fuck. He told us to piss off, leave him the car and wait for him in the local town."

."So you left him unprotected?" He turned his back and addressed the men he had brought with him, "Kill them." There was a burst of gunfire and they died before they could react. "Pile their bodies up along with that whore and burn them," he ordered.

He bent down over his Father's body and picked up the two feathers. "What are these?" he asked. There was no reply. "These must have been put here by the fucker who killed my Father. Find him and bring the piece of shit to me," he shouted. Rage etched across his face.

He turned and got back in the car and drove off into the night. The glow of the burning bodies could be seen from the rear window as he made his way back to the city. Enrique, the most powerful drug lord in Mexico, vowed he would find the man who killed his Father and make him pay, the man with the white feathers.

Chapter 4

Tim Burr had settled into his new role at MI5 and had even received a promotion. He was head of the Middle East section. The money was still rubbish but at least the work was interesting and hectic. The biggest threat to the West at the present was from ISIS and its various splinter groups. Tim's job was getting harder by the day. There had been a trend towards lone individuals, often with mental illness issues, or others with a grudge against a particular group, such as Jews or gays to carry out random attacks on these soft targets. The terror attacks were typically low tech. They would use knives, a truck or an axe as their weapon of choice and go on a killing spree.

Countering and identifying these sorts of threats, was nigh on impossible. There had been numerous attacks in England, France and Belgium and in the majority of cases the attackers had received psychiatric intervention at some time or another in their lives. These individuals were often drawn to Jihadi web sites where they would fantasise about carrying out some form of murder. Following the attacks, ISIS would then claim responsibility, even though there may have been absolutely no direct link whatsoever between the attacker and ISIS.

"How are you doing?" said Jeff Stiles, as he entered Tim's office, a big smile on his face. Jeff was Deputy Director of MI5 and worked directly with Elaine Wilkins who, when not heading up MI5, would spend a great deal of her time buying shoes.

"Not so good, there are so many potential threats. They are

rapidly outstripping the resources we have available to do deal with them."

"No, not work, how are you doing on the wedding front?"

"Oh, that is even more of a mess. I did not realise how much crap the groom has to get involved in. I don't remember doing any of this the first time round when I married Lisa.". His first wife had remarried and was now a successful business woman in her own right.

"As your best man you will be pleased to hear then, that I have solved all your problems."

"I doubt that very much but do go on."

"I have booked the meal, the VIP area at a club and the lap dancers. So there is no need to worry about anything."

"Great, you are such a help. Have you sorted anything to do with the actual wedding?"

"I have written a funny speech."

"I don't wish to appear ungrateful but I feel somehow that you have done fuck all. Have you sorted out any of the minor details you would associate with a wedding? Let's take the suit hire just as an example. Have you contacted the ushers and arranged for them and us to get measured up?"

"Shit," said Jeff

"Thought so, have you ordered the button holes or the gifts for the bridesmaids?"

Jeff looked less than confident on these matters," Of course, of course, I'll get back to you on those." He backed out the office and retreated rapidly down the corridor.

The rest of the day became a blur for Tim. A lone man in his twenties had attacked a number of people in Birmingham. No one was initially clear what had happened and so everywhere went on high alert. Reports were unclear and confusion reigned. After wasting hours of precious resources it became clear it was a drunk in an argument with a drug dealer. The mere fact that he was Arab in appearance had been enough for intelligence reports to link it to terrorist activity and trigger all the activity. Of course they had to react even though common sense would have dictated otherwise. The consequences of making the wrong judgement call could have had a catastrophic outcome. ISIS were achieving they desired goal of causing panic and fear even when nothing was happening and all the while eating up counter terrorist resources. Stretching so thin would inevitably result in the early warning signs of a genuine major attack being missed. There was, however, no choice but to treat all incidents with a full response for fear of what may happen if ignored.

Tim sat back in his chair at the end of the day and put his hands behind his head and stretched back straightening his spine, trying to get the kinks out from hunching over his screen all day. He thought of his imminent wedding and in particular Jackie and her son Daniel. At first he had been fearful of meeting the small boy and the responsibility of being in his life. After all he had no experience of children and in the main preferred to avoid them.

At first Daniel had been wary of him. That was of course to be expected, given his past experience of men, in the form of his Father, but gradually he gained confidence in Tim. Tim, in turn, gained confidence in dealing with small boys. Like Saturday when Jackie had gone shopping with her mum. He had taken Daniel to Highgate Park. They had walked through the woods and Daniel had climbed trees, then back to the Park to have a kick about. Then the forbidden fruit, as Tim took him to a burger chain restaurant which his Mother had expressly told him not to do. She knew of course that he would but it helped that Tim and Daniel shared a naughty secret and that brought them closer.

He realised that he should have left ten minutes ago. He made a quick call and handed over to the night watch. He was off for the next two and a bit weeks. He made sure he handed over every thing he was working on, before heading downstairs to the entrance. He needed to get a move on if he was not to be late for his own stag night.

In the lobby he went to his locker. On arrival all entrants to Thames House had to deposit any bags, files, keys, personal phones and laptops in their locker before being scanned and checked in. On leaving they were again checked to make sure nothing left the building without first being approved. In the past Ministers had left laptops in cabs, restaurants and bars containing sensitive and secret information on them. MI5 did not want the same happening to them.

He opened the door and retrieved the bag. It was Yosuf's bag. Tim thought back to that night Yosuf had been shot dead by the Turkish Secret service and when he had first seen Jeff Stiles. He felt sad that Yosuf had not made it. He had been a truly descent man and Tim would have loved to have had him at his wedding. They had been through a great deal together but that was in the past. With a tinge of sadness he picked up the bag which contained Yosuf's escape fund, about a quarter of million pounds in various currencies and a stack of credit cards with credit balances running in the tens of thousands.

He decided against the tube when he left the building, even though at this time of the day the traffic would be moving at a snail's pace and opted for a black cab. As the taxi crawled though the traffic he realised he would probably be late for his stag night. The taxi eventually pulled up at the depositary in Knightsbridge and he paid his fare and entered using the code he had been given on renting the box.

He knew by rights that he should have given the contents of the bag into the police, or MI5, but he felt that Yosuf would want him to do something useful with it rather than it becoming a small gift to the Treasury. He thought that he could somehow donate the money to an orphanage in Turkey. He was still haunted by the sight of the small orphaned boy with the oval eyes waiting for his abuser. He shook the image from his mind and presented his eye to scanner, to have his retina confirmed, before entering the vault.

He located his storage box and loaded the contents from the bag into it. He threw the bag in a wheelie bin before taking the tube to Leicester Square.

Jeff was already in the bar along with Elaine, their boss and a number of his other female work mates from MI5. The girls were not going on to the club, but had come for a drink and to give him a big wedding card signed by all. As they left Tim was glad he had tomorrow to recover before the Wedding, as the remaining lads started getting wasted in earnest.

Chapter 5

In Arlington Virginia, Drug Enforcement Agency Headquarters, a meeting was underway.

"Gentlemen, some information has come to light which I believe we may be able to turn to our advantage." The speaker was John D Hackensack, acting head of the Agency. He was completely bald, despite being in his early fifties. It was apparent from his clipped manner of speaking and his bearing that he had had a military background and though his hair loss was natural, he would have shaved his head in any event. Being over six foot four tall and built like a line backer, he was a formidable figure.

He looked down at the file in front of him. He liked paper files and despite the vast array of technology available, he liked his morning briefing to be in hard copy, rather than in his inbox. "As you are aware the Rojas Drug cartel is currently the biggest in Mexico. The new head of the cartel has emerged as Enrique, the son of the recently deceased Jesus Rojas. Jesus as you know was executed recently. What you may not know is that the hit was a CIA inspired affair. You realise all this is off the record."

There were three other men present and no minutes were being taken. "What was the CIA doing there?" asked Henry Jacobs. He was head of the Mexico section and again a man in his late fifties.

"I can answer that. They were, as usual, involved in an advisory capacity to the ruling government on quote, "security matters, what ever that means." At a guess they were trying to interfere in some Latin American country's government and trying to get the Mexican's do a bit of dirty work for them," said Ethan Brighthouse.

He was in his sixties and had the look of a banker. He was John's deputy and had far more tact, which meant he usually dealt with the press on anyone that needed to be treated with a modicum of civility, including the President. "In any event it went pear shaped and one of their own was tortured and eventually killed by Jesus Rojas. We all know what a perverted sadist Rojas was and he went to town on the CIA agent taking his time to torture him to death. When he had his fun he finally dumped the body outside the US Embassy with a note which warned the CIA not to fuck with him."

"The CIA were upset with this and let Rojas know that they had a bigger gang who could fuck with whom they liked," said Hackensack. "They, wishing to not be directly linked to his assassination, employed a hit man known as Annubis. We have all heard of him and his habit of leaving a white feather as his trademark on the bodies of his victims. He did the job to perfection and disappeared back into the shadows."

"I am not sure what this has to do with us?" said Brighthouse

Jacobs took up the narrative, "The President is eager to show progress on the war on drugs, something to boost ratings and show that the office is now re-energised. The war on terror is not yielding dividends in terms of progress, so we need to come up with the goods in the DEA."

David Trist spoke for the first time. He was in his early forties and usually co-ordinated the actual field activities. He was hands on and liked catching the bad guys and despite his position he had a habit of getting down and dirty with the troops on the ground. He too, was an ex-military man and looked the part, toned, fit and handsome. "So how exactly are we to up productivity, so to speak? I can assure you all that we are out there every day working our bollocks off fighting these fuckers."

"I know that, but the President needs to see it and crow to the electorate about it. We need spectacular busts, headline grabbing busts," said Jacobs.

"I have a deal in mind," said Hackensack

"You have got be fucking kidding me" said Brighthouse, "have you all forgotten the Sinoloa Cartel?"

They had been here before. A deal had been struck with the cartel whereby the Cartel were effectively immune from charges in return for which they provided information on rival cartels, which allowed the DEA to make countless seizures of drugs and successfully prosecute numerous cases. This cooperation was at its peak from 2006 to 2012 and the direct consequence of this policy was that the drug cartels had a free reign to consolidate their hold on Mexico. Now the consequences of the deals were coming home to roost. It had all come out at the US District Court in Chicago only a few years ago, when a DEA agent admitted meeting with and cutting a deal with Vincente Zambada- Niebla, the son of the Sinoloa cartel boss.

There was silence and all eyes turned to Hackensack. "I am aware of the implications."

"Aware, you are fucking crazy even to think of doing a deal," said Brighthouse

"I am not proposing a permanent arrangement just a one off trade."

"I do not believe I am fucking hearing this. Doesn't anybody learn anything around hear. Not a permanent arrangement, that's alright then. That's a bit like saying I am just going to kill somebody but that's OK as I am not a serial killer," he continued.

"Look we have to do something. The cartels are running rings around us and we look like cunts. The Country is overflowing with drugs and we look powerless. It is a one off. A straight trade, they give us enough information to boost the figures. The President gets the increased approval ratings he is looking for. We get a pat on the back and that fucker Enrique Rojas gets to torture and kill Annubis and avenge his beloved scumbag of a Pop."

"Do we know who this hit man Annubis is? Or where he can be found?" said Jacobs

"We're not that bad. I don't keep a list of assassins' phone numbers on my cell just in case I need a quick murder," joked Hackensack

"So what is the plan? If we have one that is?" said Brighthouse.

"We do have a plan. We do not know where Annubis is but the CIA knows how to contact him. So we set him up to make a hit and tell Enrique when and where. We do not set up the trap until we have milked as much information as we can from the Rojas Cartel."

"Will the CIA go along with it?"

"I have already sounded them out. It is a win, win. We get the credit for a massive increase in drug seizures, Rojas gets to avenge his Pop and the CIA get to dispose of the potential link to their murder of Mexican citizens," said Hackensack

"Yeah, win fucking win. until we are all up in front of a Congressional Hearing," said Jacobs.

"What are the options? Carry on failing?"

"I thought not. So David it falls to you to bring this home. You will be pleased to know you are going south of the border to spend some time with Rojas at his Hacienda, or as he calls it his Palace."

"Very nice, I am sure," said David Trist.

Chapter 6

Maurice Lee was on his way to the Post Office in Reykjavik. The morning air was crisp and the sky a clear shade of azure blue, the brightly coloured wood clad buildings around the harbour had an almost fairy tale appearance. The parcel was weighed and he paid for the correct postage.

Maurice had been in Iceland for a matter of seven months and was working as the Chief Financial officer at the Baltic Bank. The state of banking in the Country was dire since the 2008 crash when the government was forced to impose capital controls. These controls effectively meant that investor's money was locked in the banking system and could not be taken out of Iceland. Some nine hundred billion Kroner of foreign investor's money was tied up in this way The measures were supposed to have been temporary and the Government recently said it was getting close to lifting the restrictions, but wanted to deduct thirty five percent from any amount withdrawn, forcing Icelandic banks to pay billions of Kroner to the government.

The Baltic Bank was a private bank and was a subsidiary of a private bank based offshore. Some ninety five percent of the money locked in Iceland's banks was owed to foreigners. The Baltic Bank was offering these individuals a means of extracting funds immediately, but at a cost. In a deal with the Banking Regulator, any investor could transfer their funds to the Baltic Bank, where they would be still subject to the capital restrictions. The Baltic Bank would then loan the investor eighty percent of his funds from it parent Bank in Vanuatu. The scheme had been a success as, it effectively meant that you could get your money back, less twenty percent. The Baltic now had over six billion dollars worth of Kroner in its coffers.

Maurice had been puzzled as to why the Baltic would risk losing the further fifteen per cent of it assets, if the Government did impose the withdrawal tax of thirty five percent. The Banks stated view was that, it did not expect the tax to be imposed and would therefore make a massive profit, as they were only paying back eighty cents for every dollar they received. This had seemed a high risk strategy but, given the level of his salary, Maurice had been pragmatic in his approach and taken the job.

The Icelandic banks as a group, were pushing the scheme as hard as they could. It was a way of dumping their toxic debt onto the Baltic Bank. Within weeks it became clear to Maurice that all of this was going on, more or less, under the radar of the Regulators and Government. The scheme had been orchestrated from the start by the Vanuatu Holding Company, aided and abetted by the Icelandic bankers, allowing the Baltic Bank to get a deposit taking licence with limited scrutiny.

Money was flying into the Bank and it became clear that the Bank seemed more than happy to be facing a loss on every Kroner it took. Any risk analysis would have concluded that its behaviour was irrational, Maurice soon realised that the Bank was not at all concerned as to the potential losses it was accruing and was actively in talks with the Government, encouraging it to lift the capital controls, even if it wanted to impose the levy of thirty five percent.

Curiosity had gotten the better of him and he had resorted to his early training as an auditor and did some digging. He soon found his had his answers and he knew that he was in shit up to his neck. He could think of one solution and that was to pass the evidence to someone and let them get to the bottom of it. The parcel had been addressed to Jackie Routledge in Muswell Hill, England.

He walked up the high street and entered the small coffee shop, come chess club, come book shop and ordered some breakfast. Today was an easy day. The Bank had organised a trip onto the glacier for its newly recruited staff. He had known Jackie for years, they had trained together at Weinstock, Bradley Bird Accountants. He had a thing for her, but she was married. They had remained friends over the years, but their careers had taken different paths, he into the finance industry and she had stayed in auditing. Three months ago the Baltic was looking around for a change of auditors and he had mentioned the firm where Jackie worked. It surprised everyone, including him, when the Bank went with the idea. Her firm realistically was far too small for the job and did not really have the correct paperwork to carry out this type of role. Again, the way had been smoothed and her firm got the audit.

He looked down at the wedding invite and was pleased that he would be on the plane tomorrow and would soon see her again. He knew the terrible time she had been put through with her first husband and hoped that she had made a better choice on this occasion. His own marriage had broken down and in his heart he wished that he and Jackie could have been more than friends, but it was not to be. He looked at his watch and realised he needed to get a move on. He paid the bill and was again shocked at the cost of everything in Iceland.

He made his way to the Radisson Hotel, where just after half ten the minibus turned up. He boarded and recognised Herrick Magnus, the press officer for the Bank and two other male colleagues he did not recognise. The driver greeted him warmly and he settled back in his seat as they drove off. He had to admit the landscape was spectacular. Like Hawaii, it was one the most recent bits of land to be created on the Planet. The lava fields were still fresh and only lightly eroded by weathering. The hot springs forced steam and water to the surface. The Icelanders had harnessed the thermal activity to provide free heating and power. He was enjoying the tour.

"There are no trees in Iceland," their driver was saying, as they passed the old timber church in the middle of nowhere. Maurice had not been paying full attention to the commentary and was looking out across the black and rough terrain they were just about to head out across. There was a large plain of black and grey volcanic rocks, which they bounced across. The temperature dropped as they ascended further. The white of ice and snow began to pepper the surface.

"We are on the glacier," the driver announced. He stopped the Toyota and stepped out of the cab, "Won't be a minute."

Maurice watched as he deflated the tyres to give the truck a wider footprint and grip on the frozen snow clad surface. He climbed back in and headed straight out further onto the ice.

Soon there was only white to be seen in every direction as far as the eye could see. "It is very easy to get lost on the glacier," the driver announced. "If the wind blows the snow it becomes a white out. You can drive in circles and not know it. The only way off is to follow the sat nav, but of course you can still drive into a very big hole without seeing it," he joked.

After a further twenty minutes the truck stopped. "We should have a look," they started to disembark. Herrick went first followed by the other two and as Maurice stepped down the driver said, "Don't play with the yellow snow. It is where I had a piss the last time I was here."

Maurice took a step off to the side of the compacted snow under the wheel tracks of the van and disappeared up to his waist. He floundered trying to regain firm ground. He reached out his hand to one of his colleagues for a pull up. The blow to his face split his lip and had him seeing stars. The driver turned his back and busied himself around the other side of the Toyota.

Stunned, he was pulled up by the pair he had not met before.

33

Herrick stared long and hard at him before speaking, "We thought we made it clear when you were employed that we demanded discretion from our employees. Did we not pay you a very generous salary? Did we not provide you with a beautiful apartment?"

The slap across his face stung and his head jolted back. "That was not good enough for you. We merely wanted you to carry out your duties at the Bank. What I do not understand is that, while you were paid to carry out your job at the Baltic Bank, you decided that you would expand your role into other areas, such as checking our ultimate shareholders, our subsidiaries and sister companies, why?"

Maurice opened his mouth to answer, "I have done nothing."

"Oh! but you have, haven't you? In fact you have done quite a lot. You hacked into the Chief Executives personal files then into the holding company's files. Then you printed off all the information you gathered."

Maurice opened his mouth to speak and received a slap for his troubles.

"Please do not waste time with denials. I just require one bit of information. Where is the stuff you printed off? There are certain key documents with signatories that we really cannot have floating around."

"I did nothing"

The punch to his stomach was hard and precise. The wind left his lungs and he began to vomit and gasp for air at the same time. "Where are they?"

It took very little time to break him. A kick and a punch and his will was gone. His accountancy training was no preparation for torture at the hands of experienced thugs.

"I posted it this morning."

"For fucks sake, you really are a serious arsehole. Who to?"

Maurice realised that he was now going to put Jackie into a World of problems. He said nothing. His resolve was short lived as they continued their persuasion. "Jackie Routledge," he said

"You sent it to the Auditors?"

"To her home"

"Wanker," was Herrick's parting shot as they drove off.

On their return, they reported that Maurice had become separated and lost as the white out had come upon them. They would not find his body for another five hundred years frozen in the glacier, as it advanced inch by inch per annum.

Chapter 7

Tim had moved in with Jackie quiet soon after they got together. Now, after what only seemed like a few short weeks, they were together organising the final touches to their Wedding. The Reception was to be held in Highgate House in Hampstead. The backdrop to their wedding photos would be the orangery and the beautiful gardens. As luck would have it, there was to be an open air concert that night, so the guests would be treated to a version of the 1812 Overture, complete with a cannonade.

They had earlier gone together to pick up Daniel. Tim and Daniel had persuaded Jackie to let them go to the McDonalds on the way back. They were now back and they were all sat round the dining table putting sugar coated almonds in little boxes and tying them with decorative ribbons. They would be placed in front of each guest as they sat down for their meals at the Reception.

"Tie the bows neatly," said Jackie to Daniel.

"They are neat," he responded grumpily. It was past his bedtime and the excitement was taking its toll and good humour was giving way to irritability.

The door bell chimed and then the door to the house opened. "Only us," called Mr Routledge. John and his wife Anne, Jackie's parents, walked into the living room through the glass lobby.

"Is it that late already?" said Jackie.

"I'll give you a hand to finish these off," Anne sat down and with all hands to the pump the tying and boxing was completed in rapid time.

The plan was that Jackie and Daniel would spend the night at her parent's house. In the morning the Bride and her Father would be driven in a Rolls Royce to the Registry Office and Anne and Daniel and the Matron of Honour would follow in a separate car. Jeff Stiles acting as best man was due round to spend the night and he and Tim would make their way in a separate car in the morning.

The house phone rang and Jackie walked to the lobby and picked up the call. The conversation was brief and Jackie walked back to the dining table, as white as a sheet. "What ever is the matter?" asked Anne

She sat down and tears began to form. "What's wrong Mummy?" Daniel was becoming frightened. If Jackie cried it affected him badly, bringing back memories of his Mother bruised at the hands of his Father.

She took a deep breath. "That was Maurice Lee's sister. Something terrible has happened." Tim knew that Maurice had been Jackie's close friend for many years and that she had been really looking forward to seeing him at the Wedding. He knew that Maurice had played a part in Jackie getting to be a partner in the Accountants she worked for, as he had pushed the Baltic Bank audit her way.

"What is it, darling?" said her Father..

"He's dead." She began to sob in earnest and her mum put her arms around her in comfort. Both Anne and John were also shocked. They had known Maurice from the years when Jackie and he had trained together.

"Something happened on the way to England?" asked John.

"No, no he died in Iceland," she started crying louder. Tim picked Daniel up and sat him on his lap with his arms around him, stroking him gently, trying to keep him from panicking.

They all waited in silence as Jackie regained control and took a deep breath. "From what his sister can gather, he went on a trip on the glacier and the snow picked up. Visibility was down to a few yards and he just disappeared. They had search parties out but so far there has been nothing. He has been out on the glacier for over thirty six hours and they assume he has frozen to death."

"That's dreadful" said Anne and then lapsed into silence realising the inadequacy of her words.

"Surly with a sat nav in the vehicle they could trace it and could pinpoint within yards where he went missing and concentrate their search in that area. All he had to do was sit tight and wait?" said Tim.

"His sister asked that. It seems the sat nav had been stolen from the bus the previous night. They had to rely on the driver describing his route. They can find no trace of him, not even footprints."

She sat looking into space and silence descended. John broke the silence." Come on Daniel, big day tomorrow, let's all get a move on." Daniel got off Tim's lap and picked up his suitcase containing his toys. Jackie had dropped off his clothes earlier. He would be staying at his Grandparent's while she and Tim honeymooned.

All of Jackie's wedding paraphernalia was already at her Mum's, the dress, the Bride's maid's dresses, Daniel's pageboy outfit and something borrowed, old and blue. Tim was left with the hired morning suits for him, Jeff Stiles, his best man, and the two ushers, friends from his Uni days.

Tim helped them to the car and kissed Jackie goodnight. The next time he would see her again would be at the Registry Office.

On his own, Tim felt deflated as he stared at all the stuff lying around the house. Tim had only meet Maurice once briefly, but it still affected his mood. He realised how brief life could be. He realised he needed to buck himself up. This was no way to approach the biggest day of is life. The door bell rang at that point, breaking into his melancholy.

Jeff Stiles came bounding in full of energy as usual. "How's the condemned man?"

Chapter 8

Enrique Rojas was a very busy man today. The hippopotamuses were being delivered and he had taken charge to make sure they were settled in properly. He jumped out of the Jeep and made his way along the track leading to the large pool, that had been specially constructed with the retaining wall around it. This was a major step in the construction works he was having done in the grounds of the hacienda and a high point, the delivery of the first of the big animals.

Pablo Escobar the Colombian drug lord had built his zoo and Rojas considered him self bigger and better and so would have a bigger and better zoo. The hippos had become Escobar's legacy after his death, forming into a herd, they had taken over the countryside north of Bogotá. No one knew what to do with them until Rojas sent a team to capture a dozen of them and bring them to Mexico. There had been reluctance among the authorities for their importation. Mexico had sufficient problems without hippos wondering around attacking people. Rojas had persuaded and bribed the authorities and he now had his private zoo license.

He watched with pride as they were unloaded and took to the artificial pool he had created. He already had ostriches, antelope and had acquired four elephants from a zoo going bust in the US. He wanted lions and giraffes. He was already negotiating for the lions. The lions were being bred in Africa purely for hunting and as such were not exactly wild but he decided that they would do.

Rojas with his Father's death had free reign over the family fortune and he was spending it fast. He was determined to build a legacy and like Escobar go down in folk history. He was, of course, very unstable mentally and prone to extreme emotions. Laughing almost hysterically one minute, he could switch at the slightest provocation in to murderous rage. He was not like his Father, a sadist, but he was a sociopath. He saw himself as the only thing that mattered. He took want he wanted and only considered others as objects for him to use.

"Mr Trist is here," said the driver of the Jeep, as he clicked off the mobile phone he had just been talking on.

"Who?"

"The DEA agent?"

"Those fuckers, what could they possibly want with me, do you think well apart from my balls?" he laughed.

His driver knew enough to laugh loudly at his bosses joke.

"He can wait. Tell them to feed him or give him a girl or boy to amuse him. I need to make sure my hippos are happy before we deal with the garbage."

The driver phoned the message back to the Villa where Trist was waiting.

"Mr Rojas will be with you shortly," Rojas's butler said to Trist, "please follow me"

David Trist was feeling tired and hot. His flight had been on time and comfortable but the drive to the middle of nowhere to Rojas's ranch had been long, uncomfortable and boring. Ofcourse Rojas never experienced the discomfort and tedium of the drive, as he had plane available, or a helicopter to ferry him about. There was a landing stripe a few hundred yards from the house with a hanger at the end, housing his planes and a helipad yards from the front door.

He had to admit that the house was imposing, if not in good taste, too much, too big and too glitzy, but each to his own thought Trist. He was shown into a large library, with floor to ceiling leather bound books. On inspection he saw that they were filed aesthetically. rather than by author or subject. Big books at the bottom getting smaller as they went higher up the shelves. He causally picked one up. It was just leather bound paper devoid of type. The books were fake, just decorative.

He settled in a leather bound chair and was glad that the room was air conditioned. A young woman appeared carrying the drink he had ordered. She was a stunning girl with raven black hair. Her breasts clearly surgically enhanced were huge and forced themselves against the white flimsy silk of her blouse. Her skirt was more a belt rather than a garment and it showed, to the most advantage, her long, lithe shapely legs. Trist could not help but appreciate her beauty.

"Would you like to fuck me while you wait for Mr Rojas or I could suck your dick if you prefer?" she smiled provocatively.

Trist would very much like to have fucked her but he felt he should at least make an attempt at upholding the dignity of the DEA. "Perhaps later," he said.

"Let me know," she smiled back and left wiggling her hips. He watched he tight round bottom move side to side as she departed.

Trist was sick and tired of the DEA and the hypocritical Hackensack. As far as he could see, his boss sat on his fat arse and sucked up to whoever needed brown nosing to so he could keep his well paid cushy job. The so called war on drugs was little more than a scam, dragged out to say that something was being done to protect the American youth from the devastation wreaked on their lives, by the cheap crap flooding the streets from Columbia and Mexico. Most of the Governments whose economies were dependent on the drug trade, relied on drug money to keep them in power. If these Governments were not intentionally corrupt, most of the departments from law enforcement to procurement were.

The DEA was little better. Rather than risk failure or spend time and effort in infiltration and intelligence gathering, in a real attempt to seriously hurt the drugs trade, they would go for a quick fix, a headliner grabber.

Here he was again in the old manner attempting the quick fix, enjoying the hospitality of a murderer who was destroying the lives of Americans. He would probably get a deal with Rojas, why not? The DEA would knock out a few rival drug lords for Rojas and take the credit for the success, while clearly aiding and abetting the growth of Rojas's grip on the American drug trade.

Trist was pissed off with it. It was always his neck on the line dealing with these homicidal maniacs and he knew if the dirty deals the DEA were involved in had a light shone on them, he would be dumped by Hackensack without a second thought. The DEA would deny all knowledge and accuse him of exceeding his authority, going rogue or being corrupt. If it did not go wrong, the Government and the DEA would take the credit for their marvellous work. To make matters worse not only was he risking his neck, feeling pissed off, he was up to his neck in gambling debts.

His wife had left him and feeling fed up, he had gone with a few friends to Las Vegas. It had been a relief from life's daily shit. He had won at first and he liked it. The bug had bitten him, but all too soon he was in above his head. The pressure was increasing and the debts kept growing. He managed to do a few favours by pulling strings at the DEA and the debt would go down, but he would soon gamble it back up,

Trist's contemplations were interrupted by Rojas's arrival. "Welcome Mr. DEA," he extended his hand. Trist stood up and shook it. "I trust you have been made welcome?"

"I have."

"Let's eat." He followed Rojas through to an enormous dining room with an enormous dining table. They sat at opposite ends. Trist was glad he did not need spectacles, as he would need to have put them on to see Rojas in the distance.

The waiters were young women and topless. Rojas fondled the breasts throughout the meal and slide his hands under their skirts as they lent forward to serve. The girl who had served Trist his welcome drink was there and her breasts were even better than he had speculated. She made a point of maintaining eye contact and he could not help being aroused.

"Now what can I do for the DEA?" They were sat on the terrace overlooking the magnificent manicured gardens to the rear of the villa. The pool had the naked girls parked on Sun beds around its periphery. The girls brought their drinks to them and served them without any form of inhibition.

"We would like to offer you something you want."

"And what is that?"

"Your Father's killer," he had Rojas full attention.

"I see and in return?"

"Information on your rivals, some big busts,"

Rojas thought for a while, "It has its appeal, but and it is a big but, I do not trust the DEA. "

Trist had little to say. He knew that once Hackensack had made his splash, Rojas would get his Father's killer alright, but not in the way he expected. Annubis, the assassin, would be assigned to kill Rojas, squaring the circle and removing any link between the DEA and the drug Lord.

"I see from your expression that I am right not to trust. So how can we make this work for both of us? I think I may be able to help you on a personal level, Am I not right in that you may have a little problem with some people you owe money too?"

Trist knew this was a turning point. He knew in that instance that it was time to think of himself and stop being a pawn taking shit from the Hackensack's of the World, who never got their hands dirty, but took all the rewards.

Trist waved the young dark haired girl over and watched as she walked naked towards him. She was beautiful. "I'll have that fuck now," he said to her.

Turning to Rojas "You are right in not trusting the DEA, you would meet your Father's killer, but only when the DEA sent him to kill you. I think we can come to a much better arrangement that benefits the both of us?"

"Enjoy your fuck Mr Trist and I think I shall enjoy working with you," said Rojas.

Chapter 9

It was the day of the wedding and Tim had not slept at all well. He was definitely having last minute jitters. He was taking on a lot of responsibility with Daniel. Not only was Tim becoming a husband, he was instantly becoming a Father. He was not sure if he was grown up enough to look after himself, let alone look after a young boy. He thought the difference was that, in the normal course of events, you had nine months to prepare yourself for the arrival of a child. The adjustment period, when you realised that your life was over as you knew it and the next eighteen to thirty years of your life, would no longer be yours.

He knew he loved Jackie and he loved Daniel, but the doubts still lingered as he got out of bed at six o'clock. He looked in the bathroom mirror. He did not like what looked back at him. Rough was the only way to describe it, like a man who had not had any sleep in the last twenty four hours, which was exactly how it was.

Stiles did not help," Still time to do a runner," he said cheerily as he fried bacon.

The smell of the fry up and the nerves combined, made Tim feel sick and he returned to the bathroom, but managed not to puke. He did not usually suffer from nerves, mind you he did not usually get married either.

There was a ring on the door bell and the two ushers turned up. They were Tim's friends from Uni. They had sort of kept in touch on and off over the years. The odd wedding, birthday or party was where they came together every few years.

Geoff was a solicitor and practiced commercial law. He had therefore been of no use when Tim and his wife had been going through their divorce. Seeing him reminded him how quickly love can turn to resentment in a relationship. He put the thought out of his mind. Your Wedding Day was not the appropriate time to be contemplating divorce.

Tom was an accountant, like Jackie, but he had gone into commerce and worked for an insurance company, rather than pursue his career in the profession, as she was doing.

There was a lot of handshaking when they first arrived, followed by more warnings about the folly of getting married. This was further followed by a period of chaos and a lot of confusion as they tried getting into their morning dress. Things were too big, too small or back to front. Unlike normal clothing, formal weeding hire garments are designed to fit varying body shapes and sizes. This adaptability has the advantage for the hire company of allowing them to carry less stock. It does not have any advantages at all for the person trying to put the clothing on. For example the waistcoats, which only had fronts and no backs, could be pulled higher by tightening straps one way and pulled tighter by pulling straps another.

Geoff 's waistcoat had turned into what appeared to be a child's bib, while Stiles had managed to attach is starched collar in such a manner as to turn himself into a vicar. Tim, in his nervousness had the wrong trousers, which were three sizes too big and prompted him to do a Charlie Chaplin impersonation.

Finally, with a great deal of messing about, they managed to get dressed. Tim was now feeling far more positive, helped by the banter and humour of his best man and his ushers. "I am ready," he announced. "Insert the button holes."

There was silence then a loud "fuck" from Stiles.

BANK

"You did pick up the button holes didn't you? Tell me they are in the boot of your car?" said Tim

Stiles said nothing "For fuck's sake," said Tim.

In an instant they had gone from having plenty of time to arrive at the Registry Office on time, to not having enough time to get there at the appointed hour.

"Plan, a cunning plan, I have a plan," said Tom

It was far from a plan. Tim and Stiles would drive off to the Florists and the two ushers would head for the Registry office to meet and seat. Hopefully, Tim would appear at the wedding in time with his button hole and the bridesmaid's bouquets.

As they left, a postal van arrived with a parcel. They ran for their cars. "I need someone to sign for this," said the posty as they passed him.

"No time now, I am getting married," said Tim as he jumped into Stiles' car.

The postman did some muttering and filled out the card saying he had been unable to deliver a parcel and where and when it could be collected.

"You do realise working for MI5 does not exempt you from the motoring laws of this Country don't you?" said Tim, as Stiles raced his way across North London

"Well they sort of do," said Stiles, "I am Deputy Director of MI5 and could technically declare this an emergency."

"I am not sure I would like to test that theory in front of a Parliamentary Select Committee."

"You are probably right," he said but continued to speed anyway.

They arrived at Barnet Registry office with moments to spare. Being deputy director of MI5 did not exempt you from parking tickets when you were not on official business either. Stiles picked up a parking fine of one hundred and twenty pounds for parking in the wrong place, but Tim did get to his own wedding.

Jackie had rather a less eventful experience and arrived composed with her Father at her arm, followed by Daniel, looking as cute as a button in his tiny morning suit. The two Brides Maids completed the prossession as Tim waited nervously with Stiles to his right.

Neither of them could really remember the ceremony. It was just a blur. Tim remembered Jackie looking beautiful and Jackie remembered Tim stumbling over his vows. They kissed and they were man and wife.

The reception was full of good wishes, the odd drunk and the odd disagreement between family members. Tim had few guests. He was a little sad that both his parents had passed on. His Mum always liked a good wedding, while his Father held the cynical view that some poor fellow was giving away the rest of his life. Elaine, the head of MI5 was there with her husband, who was wheelchair bound and her son, Nicholas. She had bought herself another pair of totally impractical shoes, which she had to remove after walking nearly twenty yards.

The reception was over, in what seemed an instant and the car was waiting to take then to a hotel overnight, before they flew off on honeymoon the next day. "You have the tickets and passports?" said Jackie.

Of course he did not. In the dash to get to the florist, the travel documents were sitting on the side board in plain view so they would not be forgotten.

Tim sat beside Jackie's Dad as they drove back to Muswell Hill. Tim got the distinct impression that her Father rather thought him a bit of an idiot and was concerned for his daughter's future. "Don't worry, getting married is very stressful" he said, "no harm done."

Tim walked up the drive followed by her dad. He walked over to the sideboard and to his relief their passports were there. He checked them. The tickets were in two names Burr and Routledge as Jackie had changed her name back to her Father's and Mother's name after her divorce, not wishing to carry the brand of her abusive ex-husband around with her.

"There's an undelivered parcel card here," said her dad.

"We'll pick it up from the sorting office when we get back."

"It says here that they return it to the sender if it's not collected in eights days. Shall I collect it for you?"

"Won't you need ID or something?"

"I have done it before for Jackie when she was at work. It is addressed to J Routledge. They aren't that particular, I usually show them a credit card with J Routledge on it for John."

"That would be brilliant," said Tim

They finally let out a sigh of relief as they arrived in their room at the Gatwick airport hotel. Tim put his arms round Jackie and pulled her close. "Mrs Burr," he said as he kissed her.

Chapter 10

Mel Levy sat in his office in New York. It was a grubby one roomed office, but it was in Manhattan and just off of Wall Street. He thought back nine years when he had been one of the Masters of the Universe who could do no wrong and was the darling of Governments and Investors alike. He was an unimposing man, five foot eight inches tall with thick glasses and a slightly balding head.

Just those few short years ago he had it all, an uptown apartment valued in the millions and a beautiful house in the Hamptons. His wife had been a former Miss Arkansas and he had been on everyone's guest list, from Presidents to wannabes. He was the head man at the bank and lorded it over Wall Street. Then came the credit crunch. He knew they had been riding their luck and the bank was over extended, but money was cheap and they borrowed and took advantage. Then the money dried up as the banks tried to cover their asses. He was still that bit smarter and saw it coming sooner, so he started making sure he was not going to lose personally. The judge later called him a common thief. He, at the time, had seen it as his rightful due. So he had taken it.

He received four years in prison and the money was almost gone. What he did not pay in fines his wife took and divorced him. She had made her feelings clear as soon as the heat was on. "I do not want to be married to a loser and certainly not an ugly one at that," was her parting shot as she left.

He had two things left when he got out of prison after eighteen months. He still had his brain and he still knew some remaining potential clients that were more crooked than he - Russians. Following the intervention, by Russia in the Ukraine, American lead sanctions had been forcing a decline in the Russian economy and making it hard for the elite to launder their money. They were still siphoning wealth from the State to themselves, but were finding it harder and harder to get it out of the Country.

Levy had the solution. Prior to his career break in the penitentiary, he had been working with the Icelandic Banks to see what could be done to stave of their collapse and default. Iceland had a population of only three hundred thousand, but its banks had borrowed billions. On his release he had shown the Russians how to get their money out and laundered and at the same time giving the Icelandic banks a way out.

The scheme was simple in essence. The Russians, using a variety of companies, would open a bank in Iceland, the Baltic Bank. The Icelandic banks would allow the Baltic Bank to offer their customers the option of transferring their deposits to the Baltic Bank, who would hold them and allow the customers to free up their money by drawing down loans from Baltic Banks parent in Vanuatu. The Russian criminals got clean money in Iceland and the dirty money was used to repay the depositors. Ofcourse, the depositors only got eighty percent of their money back. Levy had negotiated with the Icelandic Regulators for the deposits to be released later in the year. The deal was, the Icelandic Treasury would need to take thirty five percent of all deposits, if its banks were to survive. Effectively the Russians would be paying fifteen percent to launder the money. The market rate was more like fifty cents in the dollar, so they were happy and Levy would be a billionaire from the commission he received of one and a half per cent from the Icelandic banks.

Things were working out beautifully and the Russians had washed six billion dollars so far. Now things were changing for the worse. Levy was part crook and part banking genius, but he had never been a murderer. The death of Maurice Lee on the glacier had frightened him. He had known the Russians were dangerous, but he comforted himself in the fact that he was only dealing with financial matters and what his clients did, did not bother him.

It all could so easily have been avoided, but the Russians, with their natural distrust for foreigners and their entrenched anti-Semitism and he being Jewish had insisted in putting one of their goons in the Baltic Bank. Through rank incompetence and stupidity the Russian had dropped the whole scheme names and all into Maurice Lee's lap. There had been no need for any of the sensitive information to be anywhere on the Baltic Bank's data base. It was pure laziness on the part of the goon in maintaining easy contact with his oligarch bosses, that had created the whole shambles.

The main problem was that the idiot had allowed the scanned documents, with the Russians' true signatures on, to get into the Bank's system. The US and the Europeans were not stupid and of course knew of the vast wealth being stolen by corrupt officials and the inner circle. But knowing and proving it in an international court is not the same.

Now, there was a dead man on the ice and a parcel somewhere in the UK, which would see Levy back inside prison and the US and Europeans seizing billions under the financial sanctions.

On the plus side the goon was out of his hair for a bit, as he had taken a plane to the UK to see if the parcel could be recovered. On the downside, Levy had a feeling that the recovery of the parcel was not going to be handled with a delicate touch.

Chapter 11

The bank of the River Nile, where the SS Misr was moored, was bustling as Tim and Jackie arrived by coach from the airport. She had always wanted to sail down the Nile, after seeing the Agatha Christie character Hercules Poirot's, adventures on a paddle steamer. Tim had found a cruise on a small twenty four cabin boat built in 1910 which had recently been restored.

"It is amazing, it looks like Poirot could be on board," said Jackie, giving him a big kiss on the cheek.

"You can see where our cabin is. Right at the front with the balcony," he pointed to the second of three decks. The top deck had a plunge pool and was surrounded by Sun beds. People where already on board. "Let's hope there are no murders."

The boats were moored three deep and they had to cross two other boats before they arrived at the reception area of the SS Misr. "Welcome, welcome, my name is George. I am here to do every thing for you. You want something, you ask George. "

The reception area was small and darkly painted with a table and chair. On one side, leading to the stern, was the dining room. Food was laid out buffet style with drinks being served by a young lad. "After you have been to your cabin, please come back here for refreshments and some useful information about your cruise," continued George.

They were shown to their cabin by another young Egyptian wearing the traditional gallibaya. "Do you usually wear that?" asked Jackie

"No, only today, I usually work in the bar and wear the usual white shirt and black trousers."

"You speak very good English," observed Tim

He smiled. "I did French, German and English at University and then a Masters in tourism, but bad timing with all the problems here. There has been a massive slow down and no jobs."

He showed them to their cabin. The room was small with a double bed, prepared with their towels folded to form a swan and rose petals scattered on the counterpane. There was a door that opened onto the balcony facing forward to the bow. They walked outside onto it. Below they could see what were obviously the cooks having a cigarette break. The balcony was just wide enough for the two small chairs and the tiny round table. The two of them could sit and watch the Nile go by in privacy, or alternatively there was, of course, the Sun decks towards the stern.

Tim opened the door to the ensuite toilet and shower. It was very compact. He had never seen a shower tray so small, or a basin that small for that matter. If you sat on the toilet your feet would be in the shower tray. "We certainly won't be showering romantically together," he said to Jackie, as she poked her head in and laughed.

There was a din from hell which made them both jump. Their helper threw the door open and began clapping, as George and two other cabin boys entered. George was carrying Champagne and glasses and his entourage were banging on drums and shouting at the top of their voices.

"Happy wedding, happy honeymoon, welcome to the Romantic Nile," shouted George, as he popped the cork and poured the champagne.

They linked arms and took a sip of the wine. "It's wonderful," said Jackie.

BANK

The boat got underway at around midnight and they stood on their balcony, as it pulled slowly into the centre of the Nile. Ahead of them were a number of cruise boats. It was almost a convoy as they made their way up stream.

"Life could not be more perfect," thought Tim, as he pulled Jackie close and kissed her.

Chapter 12

John and Anne Routledge were used to looking after their Grandson Daniel in the school holidays, but school time involved a whole different routine. Their morning started chaotically, shoes couldn't be found and pencils were missing. The project was not quite finished. Daniel had been up too late, was very grumpy and did not want to go to school, suggesting that he would learn more by going fishing with his Grandfather. His Grandfather had no intention of going fishing, which he explained five times to Daniel, before he reluctantly accepted it and agreed to go to school.

John had only done the school run a few times before and was totally unprepared for the ruthlessness that parents employed in order to get their darling little ones to school on time. He now understood why the school run chariots of choice were selected from a narrow range of motor vehicles. Anything other than a Range Rover, a Cayenne or a Jeep stood no chance of keeping the other late, harassed parents at bay. John realised, as he faced a four by four heading towards him on the wrong side of the road in order to pass the parked cars. The woman driving, with her daughter in school uniform, had no intention of pulling in to allow him to continue.

The inevitable happened and the two came face to face as he stuck to his right of way, "Get out of the way, you stupid old fat bastard." The woman was livid with rage at having her progress impeded and screamed at him.

John could not help himself and knowing he should not respond he did anyway. "Madam you are only fifty percent correct. I am neither stupid nor a bastard. I should like to point out that we drive on the left in England and you, madam, are on the wrong side of the road."

"Get out of my fucking way," she was trembling with rage and John could see she was beyond reason or humour. The pressure of getting her daughter to school, then getting to work and modern living had reduced this human being to a feral animal. John reluctantly backed his car up, while she intimidatingly drove forward, staying within inches of his front bumper and revving her engine loudly.

Finally, he reached a gap in the cars parked on the opposite side of the road to him and she could pass. She raised two fingers in the air and screamed, "Wanker," as she drove off.

"That went well," he said to Daniel.

"Mum would have punched her lights out," Daniel observed.

John decided that he would let his Anne do the school run for the rest of the period that Jackie and Tim were on honeymoon. He dropped Daniel at the school gates.

His next stop was the wedding venue. He parked up and walking inside. He checked his watch. He was on time, having fought his way through the traffic. He was surprised, but he was on time. The planner, who had organised the reception, was nowhere to be seen as he entered the lobby, where he was to meet her. He double checked his watch.

He stood there aimlessly. After five minutes, his phone vibrated and gave off the incoming text message ring tone. He took out his phone. The message was from the Wedding Planner. "Running late, be there in forty five minutes."

John could see how you could become as angry as the woman driver he had encountered earlier. Apparently, this Wedding Planner thought her time far more valuable than his. He was definitely getting old. He could not understand why people now thought it perfectly acceptable to turn up late for appointments, just because they had sent a text informing the person waiting that they were delayed. Before mobiles, if someone did not turn up within ten or fifteen minutes of the scheduled time, you left and they had the embarrassment of having to phone to apologise for wasting your time. Now you merely texted "running late" and it was supposed to be fine.

He waited for an hour until she finally turned up. "Sorry I'm late, school run problems," she said breezily without further explanation. He noted she drove a massive off roader, fully equipped for the school run battlefield.

"Glad you felt you could make it," he said pointedly.

She looked at him as if he was insane to be annoyed at being kept hanging around for an hour. "You did get my text?"

"Silly me, that makes all the difference," he said.

She was becoming angry at his comments and he realised she was just about to launch off at him. He pre-empted her, "Please just give me the items and we can be on our way."

She opened the office next to the reception desk in the lobby, "Here you go," she said.

He left carrying the bottom tier of the wedding cake, some place settings and two of the decorations as keepsakes for Tim and Jackie.

The Post Office sorting office car park was jammed with what appeared to be half of North London collecting post. He sat in the car for ten minutes waiting for some one to leave. He then had to race another driver for the space. He felt a sense of satisfaction at forcing the woman in the four by four to concede the space. Revenge for the school run incident. He was beginning to get the hang of the road wars of North London.

BANK

The queue for the post pick up window snaked out of the door and it barley moved. One Post Office worker, clearly disinterested in the whole process and moving as slowly as he could reasonably do without actually standing still, methodically and mechanically dealt with each request,

"Card," he took the card and went off through a door for five minutes.

He returned with the item, "ID."

The ID was presented and promptly ignored.

"Sign"

"Next"

Then the inevitable hold up when a change in system was required. I have three items," said one person

"Card," said the postal worker. Three cards were given. Two were given back without a word. Five minutes later he returned, "ID," He handed the parcel to the customer.

"Card," he picked up the second card and went off.

"ID"

"I just showed you my ID," said the customer

"ID," said the worker. The ID was presented and duly ignored. "Card"

This was repeated a third time. "Next"

Finally John handed over his card and after the mandatory five minute wait, the parcel of documents addressed to Jackie that had been sent four days earlier, by Maurice Lee in Iceland, had reached their destination. "ID," John handed over a credit card that was ignored. "Sign," He signed.

John made it to Jackie's house in Muswell Hill feeling like he had done a morning's hard labour. He actually managed to park outside her house on the road. Things were looking up.

He retrieved her house keys from his pocket as he walked up the short path to her door. The cherry blossom tree had shed petals all over the small front garden and the path. He thought that he would pop round before they got back from honeymoon and do a quick tidy up of the front.

He was about to put the key in the lock, but as he tried to push it home, the door just swung open. He entered cautiously and his fears were confirmed as he opened the glass inner door from the lobby to the living area. They had been burgled.

There were items strewn everywhere. Every drawer and cupboard had been opened and emptied onto the floor. Even the contents of every packet in the kitchen had been scattered onto the ground, Flour, cornflakes and even gravy granules were dumped from their respective containers.

He phoned the police. The said that they would send someone in the next few days and to make the building secure. They asked that John make a list of items that had been stolen.

He soon realised absolutely nothing was missing. Cash, TVs and Jackie's jewellery had not been taken, but had just been emptied onto the floor. The thieves had clearly been looking for something, but obviously, that something was not stuff to steal in order to sell to raise money.

John phoned and then waited for the locksmith to come and fit new locks. He decided not to spoil Jackie's and Tim's honeymoon by telling them. He and Anne would come over and clean it all up before their return. He drove home with the cake, place setting, table decorations and parcel in his boot.

Chapter 13

Trist was overseeing the operation personally. Rojas had been good to his word and the DEA had received the tip off eleven hours ago. Trist had made sure that he was hands on. So far he had his gambling debts put on hold, but he knew that he would have to deliver the hit man, known as Annubis, who had killed Rojas' Father, if he were to get his hands on the big bucks.

The airfield had been completely off the radar, built in the Everglades. It was designated on the planning at City Hall, as a parking lot for the alligator farm and air boat rides offered by the owners. On the face of it, it was a very long car park but, considering the number of tourists likely to visit at any one time, it was clearly out of all proportion to the likely needs of the purported business.

Rojas had assured him that it was a big heroin shipment and that it would boost his and the DEA's profile in the so called, War against Drugs, so beloved by the US Presidents. He looked at his watch. It was three thirty in the morning. The air was filled with the croaking of frogs and bright specs of light, in the form of alligator eyes, that could be seen watching them from the swamp. The mosquitoes formed swarms around the heads of the DEA agents surrounding the field. Despite the heavy application of deet based repellent, they did not seem to be greatly deterred from seeking out a meal among the waiting agents.

There was the sound of footsteps and he turned to see Agent Martha Swain, who was heading up tonight's raid. "They've just bagged two men in a truck. They are here to switch on the runway lights in twenty minutes from now."

"They just gave that up to you?"

"Not as such, they were just hired to switch on the lights, unload the plane and load up their truck, then deliver the drugs to an address in Miami. We offered immunity if they gave up the next link in the chain. We now know the address and bulk dealer in Miami. The two of them are pretty low level and illegal. We'll hang onto them for a few days and then export them back to Mexico," she said.

They sat in silence and waited. At first, Trist could not be sure if he was hearing anything against the chorus of night noises coming from the swamp. He strained to hear and then it became louder. The distinct drone of a light aircrafts engine.

"Switch on the strip lights," said Swain as she hurried off to join her team and a minute later the lights came on.

The strip ran parallel to the swamp. On the left were the rushes, weeds and mango trees that lined the edge of the Everglades. In the lights he could see the jetty and the sign offering trips on the airboats. He could hear the plane, but could not see it. It did not have its navigation lights on. Trist had wondered why these planes were not picked up by Air Traffic Control as they crossed the border into US airspace. He had made a phone call earlier in the day and received his explanation.

"Some are and some are not," said the controller. "They fly low and do not have transponders. The traffickers are not stupid and they have a lot of money, so they hire six or seven charter planes as decoys and literally swarm us with light aircraft. They buzz around each other and peel off. We don't have the resources to chase up on all of them. We intercept the odd one, but the profits are so vast ,they just sort of accept the odd loss of a shipment. It is like a tax to them."

The engine noise grew louder and the small plane gradually came into view. It circled the strip getting its bearings and began to descend. Trist held his breath. This was the crucial part. He hoped that the pilot's attention would be taken up with the tricky landing procedure and so not have time to check around as he came in.

The plane came in and landed heavily and bounced before settling. The plane was clearly heavily laden and it struggled to stop on the relative short, makeshift runway. It turned and taxied back and came to a halt facing into the small breeze that came in from the swamp onto the land. The truck with two DEA agents driving it, flashed its lights and headed towards the plane. The hatch opened and the pilot stepped out.

"Go, go, go," shouted Swain into the mouthpiece of her radio. The three DEA vehicles raced towards the plane with their headlights on full beam. The pilot froze like a statue, bewildered by the turn of events. He realised the game was up and lay himself on the ground with his arms outstretched. He had obviously been arrested before and knew the procedure and had no desire to get himself shot.

The Agents stepped from their vehicles and began to unload the seized drugs onto the tarmac as Trist drove over to inspect the haul. "It is a big haul," said Swain

"Fucking big," said Trist looking at about twenty million dollars worth of heroin.

The pilot was cuffed and placed in a car. The armoured truck which would be used to transport the drugs to the secure pound was on its way. It had been parked about fifteen miles away on the Interstate, waiting for a call. It was too big to conceal near the runway. For fear of it being spotted, it was decided to keep it off site.

There was an upbeat feeling of elation among the agents, a mixture of relief and excitement following the adrenaline rush of the wait and the seizure. They were clustered next to the plane, speaking excitedly and laughing.

The relative calm of the scene was suddenly shattered by a terrific roar of engines and the Agents looked around confused. For an instant they froze, their brains trying to make sense of the ear splitting din. Trist reacted first, "hit the ground," he screamed as bullets started to fly towards them from all directions.

Four air boats going full throttle came roaring from the swamp. Sat next to each driver, in the elevated seat, which was directly in front of the engine and the propeller, that pushed the boats skimming on the surface of the swamp, stood a gunman, spraying bullets, from a small Uzi machine gun.

The agents scrambling for cover were taken unawares and struggled to bring their own fire arms to bear on the men that had now jumped from the boats and were intent on recovering their drugs. Swain was hit, as were two other DEA agents, as they began to return fire, forcing the approaching men to fall to the ground for cover. The agents were out numbered and out gunned. It was only a matter of time before the assailants got the upper hand and recovered the drugs and made off into the night in their air boats. Once in the backwaters an army would not be able to find them.

Trist wondered if this had not been a deliberate set up, but realised Rojas, nor any of the other drug lords making these shipments, could know what arrangements the buyers had made to protect their investment. The suppliers were only responsible for delivering the heroin, after that it was up to the distributor to process and sell it into the US market. In any event, his operation was going badly wrong.

Just as it appeared that all was lost, the armoured truck appeared and drove up on the six gunmen from behind. The driver, seeing the situation had driven the truck up onto the runway with the lights off. He drove at high speed at the men, switching his lights on, highlighting them in the main beam. Four guards in full body armour jumped from the truck and began spraying the would be highjackers with bullets. They were now caught in a cross fire between Swain's team at the aircraft and the newly arrived armoured truck.

Silence, apart from the groaning of the injured, one dead and two wounded. It was a bad night for the DEA. It was no comfort that all but one of the drug dealers had been killed.

"That was fucking close," thought Trist as he drove away. He certainly had to earn his money.

Chapter 14

Douglas is the Capital of the Isle of Man, a tiny island with a population of about sixty five thousand people. Situated between England and Ireland, its claim to fame is the Isle of Man Tourist Trophy motor bike races. The other thing it is famous for is it lack of corporation and capital taxes. While it has a tiny population, the advocate's offices, in Athol Street, have their walls covered in brass plaques bearing the names of thousands of corporations who have their registered offices on the island. One of those companies was Baltic Bank Holdings

Mel Levy had just arrived at Ronaldsway airport, having flown from New York to Gatwick in England and then onto the Isle of Man. He sat in the taxi, looking out the window. He had never been to the Island before, but had established hundreds of companies there to help his investors minimise their tax bills. This time, he wished he had not suggested to the Russians the possibility, of not only laundering their money for them, but having cleaned it, of taking it tax free. Because of this, he now found himself on a tiny island in the middle of the Irish Sea meeting three of the most dangerous and powerful men in the World.

"Do you notice there are no trees," the taxi driver interrupted his thoughts.

"What?"

"There are no trees," repeated the cabbie. "Well, there are trees but no naturally occurring ones."

Levy wondered if that was true or not. "Why is that?" he asked

"No idea," he replied.

Levy was getting a sense of the Manx character and made a mental note to avoid, as far as possible, conversation with taxi drivers during his brief visit.

"The Manx cats have no tails."

Levy knew he was going to regret this, "Why?"

It was the mistake he thought it would be, "I have no idea. Odd isn't it?"

"The Fairies live her under this bridge," he said as they rounded a bend. "You should make a wish."

Levy did, but it clearly failed as the driver did not spontaneously combust. The drive continued to the Advocate's office, but not before Levy had learned that the Manx flag had three legs, so you could never fall over.

Pelham Stevens were a well known firm of Manx Advocates who specialised in offshore work. Levy had used them on numerous occasions before, to set up special purpose companies, as they were known, to mitigate his and his client's potential tax liabilities. This was the first time he had, however, met Gerald Pelham face to face.

"Welcome to the Isle of Man, Mr Levy. It is so good to put a face to a name after all these years."

Levy knew, of course, that Pelham was just being polite and discreet. After all, Levy's face was known thoughout the World as the rogue banker that was fined a billion dollars and sent to prison for four years.

"Your colleagues have just arrived and are in the conference room. Would you like coffee?"

Coffee sorted, he was shown into a large room with a central table and eighteen chairs around it. Five of the chairs were occupied. Two of the men seated were clearly body guards, Levy knew them, Andrei and Vadim. They were ex Romanian Special Forces and lethal, you would never mess with them knowingly.

The other three were typical, middle aged, successful businessmen types. Of course, their success was built less on their business acumen, but more on fraud, corruption and theft. Ultimately, their success was built on the closeness to their association to the Kremlin.

The level of corruption and theft is so vast, that it actually becomes a problem for the powerful elite at the top of the Russian political establishment. The only way to survive is to stay in power, in power forever. It was alleged that Boris Yeltsin, the first Russian Premier had stolen so much for his friends and family, that he knew if he lost power, the new ruling clique would have had them all disposed of, in order to steal the money back for themselves. When the new President came to power, it was rumoured that he did a deal with Yeltsin and his cohorts. They supported him and in return he would not have them killed when he moved into the Kremlin.

"Gentleman, as you know, under Manx law we, as lawyers are required to know who our clients are. The reason is to crack down on money being laundered and possible terrorist funding. As part of the "Know Your Client" procedures, we need to see your passport and verify your address. Once we have done that, we can move to the Company meeting and the distribution of the dividends."

The first businessman handed over his passport. Pelham took a look at the passport. It was French. The next two were Estonian and Dutch.

He looked down at the three passports and supporting documents, none of which bore any resemblance to the men sat around the table. "These do not appear to be your passports?"

"I think if you look more closely you'll find that is exactly what they are," replied one of the three.

Pelham was beginning to feel nervous. He was used to dealing with all forms of tax avoidance and tax evasion over the years, but he had never encountered such a blatant level of rule flouting. "There are only three passports here," he said, buying time to think.

Vadim got up from his seat and placed a large metallic case on the table in front of Pelham. "Please to open," he said.

Pelham opened the case. There was the forth passport. There was also ten million dollars, neatly bound in packets.

"I think that satisfies any outstanding questions you may have," said another of the businessmen.

While not being the most honest of men, Pelham did feel torn. It was a lot of money and he certainly had all the tools at his disposal to launder the ten million dollar bribe and get it legitimately into his hands tax free. On the other hand he would be crossing a line into pure fraud.

"I see you are a man of principle. The man whose passport, you have in the brief case, the CEO of our little enterprise, understands men of principle. You may have heard of Alexander Litvinenko. He was a man who held strong beliefs and his principles forced him to speak out. I think you know the consequences of holding too many principles."

Pelham now realised that this money went all the way to the Kremlin and he knew what had happened to Litvinenko. He died a horrible death, when he was poisoned with a radioactive isotope traced back to the Russians.

Choice made for him, Pelham said, "Thank you Gentleman, that seems perfectly in order."

He moved on to the next order of business. "Their being a quorum we can now hold a board meeting to approve the payment of the dividends to the following members," he handed out a sheet of paper showing just over sixty million dollars to be transferred into various bank accounts, in such Countries as Belize, the Virgin Islands and the Cayman Islands. The payments were unanimously approved.

"Mr Levy, will you accompany me to the Bank where I have an appointment set up. I will present the necessary documentation and with your signature, we shall make the transfers."

"We will have a meeting here and wait for Mr Levy." Pelham and Levy left to take the short walk to the bank.

On their own, the three Russians looked towards Vadim. "You burgled this woman's house, Jacqueline Routledge and could find no trace of the parcel sent to her by Maurice Lee?"

"Nothing, there was no trace of it."

"Then we have no choice. We need some leverage over her. You and Andrei will go to London and take control of the matter."

"We have a problem, her husband"

"Why is he a problem? They are away on honeymoon in Egypt, nowhere near London"

It is not where he is. It is who he is. He is MI5," said Vadim, "That is why we found it so difficult to find any information on him. Russian Intelligence have checked him out and come back to me with his background and they confirm that he is secret service."

"We shall have to take care of it. OK Vadim, you go to London and Andrei it looks like you are off to Egypt"

"We do not have enough personnel to do it," said Andrei.

"Use contract personnel, not ideal I know, but we cannot directly involve the Russian Secret Service. It is too delicate a moment. We are making progress with the West in getting the sanctions eased, we do not want an incident that goes straight back to the Kremlin."

Levy joined the five of them as they walked back to the Sefton hotel, where they were spending the night, before flying off to their respective destinations. Being several millions each the richer, the Russians were in a bit of a holiday mode.

"I like the trams with horses and the policemen look so nice here in their hats and white uniforms," commented one before licking his ice cream

They all agreed that the Manx police, in their summer uniforms, were vastly smarter looking than their leather jacketed Russian counter parts.

"Is Pitkin," shouted Vadim, almost ecstatically.

"Yes, yes is Pitkin."

"No it cannot be. Yes it is, it's Pitkin"

Levy could not understand what was happening. The two goons were jumping up and down like excited children at the sight of a life size bronze of a small man with a cap, sitting on a bench under a street light.

They started taking selfies, then photos of each of them in turn sitting on the bench. Then Levy was asked to take a group shot of them all with the statue. All the while they were laughing and saying Pitkin.

When they finally stopped, Levy bent closer and read "Norman Wisdom". He had lived on the Island and died there aged ninety five, in his home Ballasella. He had never heard of the comedian, famous for his many films with his character Pitkin, a cheeky chap, who things never quite worked out for. The Romanians had. He was a national hero.

Chapter 15

"How was the school run today?" Anne Routledge asked her husband John.

"Carnage, I did not realise getting Daniel to and from school would be so stressful. We should have insisted on Jackie doing a risk assessment before she went on honeymoon." It was getting on for nine o'clock in the evening and Daniel should have been in bed, but his grandparents indulged him and he was just finishing a computer game on his Play Station.

"Time for bed soon, can you finish up now?" she said.

Dragging his feet Daniel went to bed. It was nearly half past nine before they sat down in front of the television. "It is nice having him here, but I am glad we can give him back at the end of the day," said Anne.

"I think we've done our bit bringing up kids. I hate to say it but we are getting a bit too old and I don't have the energy anymore," said John.

He had just sat down and was about to lift his cup of tea to his lips when there was a knock on the door. "Oh no," he said.

"Don't worry I'll go. It will only be charity requests, or Jehovah's Witnesses."

Anne opened the front door and he heard voices. Suddenly the living room door opened and Anne flew into the room and fell to the ground as she was pushed violently by a large man wearing a balaclava. A second man followed them in. John started to get up and a gun was pointed in his face. "Don't move," said Vadim.

The second man pointed his gun at Anne and she pulled herself up from the ground "Sit bitch," he screamed

Vadim was not at all happy with his helper and would have preferred Andrei. On getting to London, he had to make do with whoever he could get for hire at short notice. He had got hold of the pair, Boris the Serb and Ivan the Terrible, two wannabe big time gangsters, from the Russian club in Soho. Boris was the screaming idiot with him in the Rutledge's front room and Ivan was waiting just down the road in the car. The more he thought about it, the more Vadim was convinced that hiring these two young hot heads was not going to turn out well.

"For fuck's sake, stop shouting and waiving your gun about," he said.

"What do you want?" said John. He could feel his heart pounding.

"Where is the boy?" asked Boris.

Anne and John looked at each other, neither answered.

Boris went to strike John. "Stop that. We are here to do a job not beat up old men. The boy is obviously in bed. Just go up and get him," Vadim said.

Vadim could hear doors smashing open and screaming. "For fucks sake, they could not have made more noise if they tried," he thought.

Daniel's memories of his Father coming back drunk rushed into his head. When the gunman entered his bedroom and pulled him from his bed he thought he was to get a beating as his Father had done and he knew the only way to avoid it was to run. Most children being dragged from their bed would have frozen with fear. Daniel's thought was of only one thing, flight.

BANK

Boris dragged Daniel into the living room. Vadim turned to look and in that brief second Anne, screaming in a frenzy of pure protective instinct, jumped from the chair and threw herself at Boris, clawing, kick, punching and biting. Daniel kicked and bit and Boris loosened his grip and Daniel ran screaming from the room and out the front door.

Vadim was hit by John, who had thrown himself at him. John was no fighter, but this was his grandson. He may not have been a fighter, but he did weigh over nineteen stones, of mostly fat. He struck Vadim flat out in a rugby tackle and Vadim lost balance and hit the floor.

Anne was clinging to Boris's legs and stopping him chasing Daniel. He pointed the gun and fired. She lay still.

Vadim and John stopped, both shocked by the sound of the gun. "What the fuck are you doing," screamed Vadim, as Boris turned and pointed his gun at John, "Stop."

Vadim used the pause to punch John stunning him and grabbing Boris by the arm, pushed him into the street. Vadim could hardly believe the situation they were in. He felt like shooting Boris himself. All the idiot had to do was go upstairs and snatch a small boy from his bed, Instead he had smashed his way about like Arnold Schwarzenegger, playing the Terminator and now they were in the middle of the street with half the road out, looking at the commotion.

The boy had gone. John was screaming for help from the doorway. Boris turned and fired at him. He fell but continued screaming for help. Ivan lost his nerve at the sound of gunfire, screaming and the neighbours opening windows and doors and drove off like a lunatic, leaving Vadim and Boris to their own devices.

The sound of sirens was fast approaching and three minutes later a police helicopter was overhead. Vadim knew they were fucked. London was on high terrorist alert and nearly three hundred armed police were on the streets ready to deal with any threat. In Paris, a few armed ISIS inspired gunmen had roamed around, killing people at will. London had learnt from this and would muster and deploy specially trained officers to an incident within minutes.

They ran toward Pinner High Road looking to highjack a car. The helicopter was above them and Vadim knew it was pointless, but ran any way. There were no cars moving. The area had been sealed. They stood in the middle of the abandoned street. It was so silent, it felt as though time was standing still.

The silence was shattered. "Armed police lay down your weapons," the command came through a loud hailer.

Boris screamed as though he was some sort of animal and began shooting. Vadim's last thought, before they both died in the return fire was, "What a fuck up."

Chapter 16

"Gentlemen, I should like to open this meeting with a little pat on the back for all of us. The White House is more than happy with our recent successes in the War on Drugs," said Hackensack. It was a hot day in Arlington Virginia and it was warm in the meeting room, despite the efforts of the air-conditioning. There were no jackets or ties around the table today.

David Trist picked up the narrative. "As you all know we have been co-operating with the Rojas drug syndicate in this matter. The first shipment we intercepted was in Florida. It was a shaky start with a fully fledged gun battle. However, the shoot out actually was beneficial to the image of the DEA. The press picked up on it and portrayed us as modern style heroes. As they say Gentlemen, all publicity is good publicity and that seizure really upped the Agency's profile nationally."

Henry Jacobs raised his hand slightly to gain the floor, being in charge specifically of the curtailment of the Mexican drugs industry, he felt he should make an interjection. "The first seizure in Florida was of drugs being shipped by the Rojas Syndicate. After the first couple of drug busts, it would be obvious to the drug Cartels that one of their number was ratting them out to the DEA. Rojas made sure he was not suspected, by setting his Cartel up for a big hit."

"Since then he has given up eight more massive shipments and some of the Cartel members have been hit multiple times. We are beginning to cause them real pain," said Trist.

"One Cartel member, Oscar Perez Rodriguez has not been

targeted at all by Rojas," added Jacobs.

"He is Rojas' biggest rival and Rojas has made sure that all the suspicion falls on him as the potential DEA informant. If Rojas could make the other Cartel members turn on Rodriguez, then it would consolidate his supremacy as the chief drug lord."

"Now he wants his reward. He wants the assassin, Annubis, who killed his Father and he would like us to arrange the assassination of Rodriguez using Annubis. He then plans, with our help, to capture him after he has killed his main rival," said Hackensack.

Brighthouse spoke for the first time," We can't go along with this, surely?"

"We can to a point," continued Hackensack. "We can certainly facilitate the death of Rodriguez, but it would be no bad thing if the same happened to Rojas. We'll instruct this Annubis to kill them both."

"There is one small problem, is there not?" said Jacobs, "Annubis is a CIA asset and they do not seem to want to hand him over for our use."

Trist knew he had to somehow manoeuvre himself into control of this situation. The pious bastards sat round this table were only interested in their political careers and fattening their bank balances. They were sat round this table openly discussing murder, with a total disregard for the legality of it and with not a second thought for the judicial process. Neither Rojas nor Rodriguez had been anywhere near a court, yet their death sentences were being engineered by the group gathered here. In essence Trist was justifying his betrayal of the DEA to Rojas by condemning their hypocrisy, by overlooking his own. At the end of the day, Trist was just greedy and wanted the fortune offered to him by Rojas.

"I have made overtures to Langley," interrupted Trist.

"I am not sure I authorised any approach," said Hackensack. "In any event, I certainly do not remember asking you to get involved."

"It was informal," Trist continued, he had to cast the die and get control of the operation if he were to be a rich man. "I put the matter to them in a different manner."

"How?" asked Jacobs.

"I requested co-operation from them for myself in the form of their assassin."

"You volunteered to work for the CIA?" said Hackensack in almost total disbelief.

"Sort of, I pointed out that our interest coincided. Their brief and interest in Mexico extend much further than the drugs trade. In fact the income generated into the Mexican economy by the drug Cartels are vital to the Government there although, neither they nor the CIA, could openly acknowledge that fact. Key among the issues that concern the US administration is the level of migration and social tensions it is causing. In essence they need the drug money, but could do without the control and influence exercised by the drug lords."

"So you volunteered us to work with them in intervening in the politics of Mexico?"

"I volunteered to take down two drug lords that are responsible for addicting and killing millions of American kids with their cheap drugs," said Trist.

"Let's take this down a notch, before tempers are lost," said Brighthouse.

Hackensack took a deep breath. He was seething that Trist had usurped his authority in having direct dealings with the CIA. His brain, however, was working overtime, wondering how he could take credit if it turned out well and how he could distance himself and pass the buck if it went tits up. "Go on," he said.

"They will lend us their asset in the form of this contract killer, Annubis, but we have to take the rap if the murder of Mexican citizens comes out. They do not want the shit to come back to them if it gets out."

"So they insist that the operation on the ground is run by us?" asked Jacobs.

"Yes and I offered my services as our man in the field." In fact the reverse was true, but Trist had to be there if he were to make good his promise to Rajas of delivering his Father's killer's head to him. It had been tense with the CIA, they were very reluctant to let Trist be out in Mexico with a gun in his hand and a contract killer. Somehow he had managed to convince them to go for it. They would give him access to Annubis's services and he would make sure the CIA was in the clear. Of course, the costs would come out of the DEA's budget. That fact had been the deal clincher.

Even Trist had to admit the whole thing made little sense for the CIA or DEA, but he had done the ploy of telling the CIA that it was what the DEA wanted. Now he was telling the DEA that it was the CIA's idea. Of course all he wanted was to get his payoff from Rojas, so he did not care as to the sense of it.

"There doesn't seem to be a downside," said Jacobs.

The rest of them nodded. Like most decisions in the end it was not a decision at all. Someone came up with something that appeared not to have any real downside and so no one actually vetoed it. They group round the table were all now focused on how they could take credit if it went well.

"Alright, go to Mexico, take you assassin and don't fuck up," said Hackensack.

Chapter 17

Jackie and Tim were aboard the paddle boat moored back in Luxor. Their cruise down the Nile had been relaxing and enjoyable. The sights of Ancient Egypt were invocative and romantic. They were in love, relaxed and happy. They woke up however feeling a little apprehensive. Despite recent crashes, deaths and health and safety issues they had booked, against their holiday representative's advice, a hot air balloon trip along the Nile.

They were up early and were the only people from the SS Misr that had decided on this particular excursion. "Do you think it is safe?" Jackie was having last minute doubts as they waited on the quayside.

"It is all a matter of degree. It is safer than base jumping and more risky than lying in bed," said Tim.

"You mean no," said Jackie.

"I mean it will be exciting and spectacular."

"And dangerous?"

"Probably."

Before Jackie had time to talk herself out of it the mini bus turned up and they were loaded aboard. There were four other couples on board as they set off. The balloon trip commenced somewhere on the left bank and the bus set off at a break neck pace through Luxor.

"I may have underestimated the danger of this particular

excursion. In all probability we shall die in a car crash long before we get to the launch site," said Tim.

Jackie was not seeing the funny side as the bus nearly mowed down a couple of pedestrians. Clearly they were running a bit late and as the driver's only job was to deliver the punters to the launch area, he was determined to arrive on time. It appears that he did not consider it part of his remit to deliver them alive or even in one piece.

The mini bus turned off the road onto a gravel track and headed off into the sandy desert landscape. Tim feared he would sustain irreparable spinal injuries as they raced along, hitting divots and rocks at full pelt. In the distance was a cluster of balloons, five or six in total. They were surrounded by a group of Egyptians pulling ropes and herding people.

They screeched to a halt and were ushered speedily from the bus. Some of the balloons were already airborne and rising high into the sky. It was a scene of total chaos, filled with milling tourists and shouting Egyptians. Tim was beginning to have real doubts as to the competence and organisation of the whole thing and started to think they should not have dismissed the holiday reps advice so perfunctorily.

The balloons were enormous and the baskets held about twenty people. The basket was divided into sections and four people were squeezed in each. In the centre was the pilot.

"English, Deutsch, Francais?" asked a ground crew member approaching them in a hurry.

"English," replied Tim

"Please, quick to follow," he set off in the direction of one of the balloons.

They jogged behind their guide to a red and white balloon with eight men clinging to ropes as the pilot blasted hot air from the burner into the canopy. "In quick, in," he shouted.

Jackie was pushed into the basket landing upside down in a sector of the basket with another couple already aboard. Tim entered in the same unceremonious manner. Hardly had they got themselves the right way up when the ropes were released and they began their ascent.

"Welcome, ladies and gentlemen, I am your pilot." Tim looked across to see a young Egyptian wearing Aviator Sunglasses and looking every bit a Tom Cruise look-alike from "Top Gun".

"I am a commercial airline pilot, so rest assured you are in the very best of hands. You are all English, yes?" This was confirmed.

""Safety first, one do not fall out of the basket. Two, most importantly, don't let me fall out of the basket," he laughed as he turned up the burner to increase their assent.

Suddenly the traffic noise was gone. The frantic hustle and bustle of the launch site was far below them. The silence was intense. It was so peaceful and beautiful, the sky deep blue above and the Sun shimmering red, gold and orange on the horizon as it began its daily rise in the east.

Jackie was enthralled as she looked over the edge of the basket at the miniature scene below. The Nile stretched as far as the eye could see in both directions. The tourist boats could be seen making their way along it. Other boats from the small to large cargo vessels all moved silently along. All was so quiet and peaceful, they just stared and hugged each other.

Tim became aware that the other balloons had blown off along the bank of the Nile, but theirs was being blown out over the river. "The wind has changed," said the pilot, "You are lucky you are crossing the Nile. Usually the wind blows us up along one side. You are special and going for a better ride."

They drifted serenely over the Nile, the life blood of Egypt. They could see, even in the modern era, how the agriculture and buildings were spread out along its banks in a narrow strip. Beyond that the vast expanse of arid shrub and sand stretched for miles into the distance.

They continued their quiet sail along and across the Nile passing fields and trees below on the opposite bank. "We need to find a place to land," said the pilot. They had been in the air for just over an hour.

He vented the balloon and it began to descend, slowly at first. It soon became apparent that landing may not be as simple as the pilot was leading them to believe. There were buildings, trees and fields full of crops, such as sugar cane.

Their descent became more rapid and it was plain that the wind was moving them along more swiftly the closer they approached the Earth. The pilot was doing his best to avoid obstacles, but his influence on the balloon's path was limited. They skimmed the first of several trees but crashed into the next cluster. The balloon bounced off and continued to descend. There were a few gasps as more trees loomed even closer.

The pilot deflated the balloon further and the hit the ground with a bump. It did not come to a stop but continued to be blown, dragging the basket behind it across a field. Tim found himself lying under Jackie and the other couple, as the basket fell onto its side.

The next thing he realised was that he and another four passengers had been tipped from the basket into a field of very spiky cut sugar cane. He struggled to his feet to see that the balloon, still containing the other twenty passengers including Jackie, had risen up into the air. With the sudden loss of ballast in the form of Tim and the three others, also dislodged into the field, it was off again.

He gave chase and watched as the balloon deflated further and crashed again. It was dragged along for a about fifty yards, giving the passengers a very bumpy ride. There was a roar of engines and horn tooting as a truck load of Egyptians arrived. The ground crew had raced over the Nile and tracking the balloon from the ground had caught up with it.

They secured the balloon and the rest of the slightly unnerved passengers were helped out. They were shepherded to the road side where a mass of small children appeared as if by magic and started asking for money. Drums also appeared from nowhere and the usual cacophony ensued as they waited for the minibus to turn up. Tim was fascinated by the metal drums that seemed to be made for industrial grade metal ducting and weighed a ton. He could not understand how they just appeared. Did the locals just carry them around all the time in the hope of deafening some unsuspecting tourist?

They bus turned up and they were driven back to the SS Misr. It would appear that having not managed to kill them by crashing the balloon, they were doing the best to finish the job in a road traffic accident.

"Well that was different," said Tim giving Jackie a big hug as they stood on the quayside.

George came rushing off the boat. "Please, please you must phone this number," he shouted running down the gangplank.

They were in shock. "At least Daniel is OK," said Tim in a vain attempt to comfort Jackie.

They had learnt of the attack on Jackie's Mum and Dad. Jackie was stunned and almost hysterical. Tim and the rep had been frantically phoning the airport and had finally secured their passage back to the UK. The first flight they could get on was at nine that evening.

The wait was agony and the honeymoon and even that morning's balloon trip now seemed of another time and place.

Chapter 18

The private helicopter set down on the helipad aboard the Lady Heloise tied up in Monaco. The owner, Sokolov Yerik had only actually set foot on the yacht once before, when he had taken delivery of it. He had flown in that morning to Nice and taken his private helicopter from the airport to Monte Carlo. The yacht had a full compliment of crew, captain, gourmet chefs and today, twelve heavily armed security personnel.

Although Yerik was in the league of supper rich he still chartered the boat and the income added to his vast fortune. A month ago the boat had been rented to a Turkish trade delegation for the Monaco Grand Prix race week. That week alone had added over a million dollars to his income.

"Nice boat," he said as he alighted from the helicopter. "I forgot how pretty it was." He surveyed the boat and looked at the town of Monte Carlo. It truly was a fabulous place and no taxes added to its appeal. "I must try and come here more often. It is so much nicer than Moscow."

Yerik had been a close friend of Russia's President and they had worked together in State Security. They were a close group, Vasiliev Nikhil and Volkov Lesta had all also demonstrated their loyalty to the Kremlin. A few days ago the trio were together in the Isle of Man and today the other two were on board waiting for Yerik in the state room.

"Comrades, nice to see you all again so soon," said Yerik as he entered the magnificently burr walnut panelled room with its deep leather chairs drawn up around the flame mahogany table.

There was not a happy atmosphere as they sat down to a late breakfast of coffee, caviar, smoked salmon, bacon and croissants. Lesta was particular agitated as Yerik drew up a chair and sat himself down. "What the fucking hell, happed?" he said

"A fucking fuck up happened," said Nikhil

"Gentlemen, gentlemen there is no use in crying over spilt milk. We have to deal with the reality."

"But what a mess, Vadim and some idiot he hired to help, dead. Newspaper headlines, press and half of the British police and Secret Service trying to find out what is going on. How fucking hard can it be to abduct a small kid from two old age pensioners?"

"Harder than you would think, apparently," said Yerik.

"It is not funny," said Lesta, "Those papers with our names on are still out there somewhere and in case you forget,. it is not just our signatures on these papers. Unless we all want to end up glowing in the dark with radiation poisoning, we had better sort this out and fucking sort it fast."

"The plan was so simple. It beggars belief that it so badly screwed up. What was that wanker's name, Maurice Lee? He posts the evidence to this accountant woman, Routledge. We search her home while she is on her honeymoon and find fuck all."

"Then we try to get hold of her kid so when the documents turn up we have her under our control. Now we have a couple of old age pensioners in hospital and fucking dead bodies all over London, fucking wonderful," said Lesta

"Well at least the documents have not made their way into the Americans' hands and our money has not been seized or frozen."

"Well for now, but it's only a matter of time before this Routledge woman turns up with the evidence and we are fucked," said Nikhil

"There is also the matter of her new husband, he is MI5 and I am guessing he is probably not happy with us after the debacle with his stepson and will be even less happy if we fuck with his brand new wife," said Lesta.

"We have no choice, we have to retrieve the documents or we are all dead men."

"We can only assume that she has the documents somewhere and for some reason has not acted on the information, yet. Yet being the operative word, she will act though. "

"I think that her wedding was the distraction. But you are right, when she gets back she will undoubtedly act. After all she is the lead auditor for the Baltic bank. Then my friends as they say, the game will be up."

"We will have her here soon and her husband will be dealt with, rest assured," said Yerik.

Chapter 19

Jackie and Tim had packed their cases and were alone on board the SS Misr, except for the crew. The other passengers were on an excursion visiting the temple at Luxor. George had been fussing around them most of the day and was overly attentive to their needs. Finally, it was time to go to the airport and take their flight back to the UK.

"We'll bring the luggage, do not worry," said George.

"Jackie began to walk up the gangplank to the car and Tim was just about to follow, "Mr Tim," said George.

Tim stopped to see an agitated George chasing him. Tim thought he may have forgotten something and stopped.

"Yes?"

George had a small bead of sweat forming on his top lip and looked very nervous. "Mr Tim we are concerned about you and hope that all will be well when you get home."

Tim was anxious to catch up with his wife and turned to go, "Thank you."

George stepped in front of him and Tim was forced to stop, "Please," he said. "I am in a hurry," he was becoming annoyed at George's excessive concern.

"Of course," said George and finally moved to the side allowing Tim to pass.

It was of course too late and George's delaying tactics had served their purpose. Jackie had reached the end of the gangplank and was walking towards the waiting taxi when three men rushed forword, grabbed her and started dragging her towards a waiting Mercedes.

"Tim, Tim," she screamed "help."

Tim became aware of the disturbance and saw Jackie putting up a struggle on the quayside with her assailants. She was not going easily and scratched, kicked and managed to break free briefly. She tried to run back towards the SS Misr and Tim, who was running up the gangway.

The three men caught up with her. Two of the men started dragging her back towards the waiting car. The third headed towards Tim to block his rescue attempt. The third man was Andrei, the Romanian and Tim could see that this man would not be easy to overpower. Tim despite his years of martial arts training had only employed his sport in the real World once before and that was the night he had meet Jackie, dealing with a couple of drunks that were molesting her. Now it looked like he would need to fight once again to save her. Andrei was not a drunk outside a nightclub. It was clear that he was altogether a different proposition. He was a professionally trained in the military.

Tim just ran at him full tilt. Andrei was not, however, interested in delaying his departure from the scene and Tim realised too late that he was armed. In that instance he saw Andrei level his automatic pistol straight at his face.

Tim knew that he was going to die and there was nothing he could do to prevent it. He saw Andrei's expression was one of irritation and annoyance. He was treating killing Tim as an inconvenience that needed to be dealt with so he could just get on with his task of kidnapping Jackie.

Annubis looked down the sight of the snipers rifle as Jackie had walked up the gang plank. She was not his target. No, he had been employed by Andrei to deal with the husband. Normally he would receive more information on his targets, a photo, name and often details of their daily routine. On this occasion there had been no time. Andrei had hired his services before and had been in a rush. The Russians were short of man power and the whole thing had been last minute. The Russians knew the woman's name, Jacqueline Routledge and that she was on honeymoon with her husband Tim. They knew that Tim worked for the British secret service but knew little more. Annubis' brief was simple. kill the husband and stop him interfering in Jackie's abduction.

He saw the figure start to run up the gangplank and one of the abductors turn back to stop him. He trained his riffle on the husband and brought his face into view, his finger curling round the trigger.

Tim's face appeared in the scope. Annubis knew that face. He froze shocked. This was a man, probably the only person in the World, he would not kill. This was that man that had helped him get justice for the murder of his young innocent brother. The man that night in Jason Delonge's flat he had met, who was there, prepared to kill for him.

In that instant he made his decision and fired.

Tim was shocked. He had expected to die. The gun in Andrei's hand was pointed straight at his face. He could see the fingers begin to contract, in that instant he knew that his life was ended.

Andrei crumpled at his feet. His head had simply exploded. The bullet from Annubis' rifle was full metal jacket and had fragmented on entry into the skull and literally blown his head in two. Tim was spattered with blood and brains. It covered his face and front to his waist. For an instant he failed to understand what had occurred and thought he was witnessing his own death as an out of body experience.

He recovered and chased after the two men still dragging Jackie along the pavement. She was still struggling. In desperation to speed up progress, one of her attackers punched her. She slumped, unconscious. They were under strict orders not to harm her. She would be no use to the Russian oligarchs dead.

He saw her pushed, dragged no longer, struggling into the car. The wheels squealed as it accelerated away. Tim was running flat out in an attempt to catch the car. His path was suddenly blocked by the security police that patrolled the quayside in droves to protect the tourists from possible terrorist attack. Their discipline was suspect. Tim had often seen them idling on the side of the river, smoking with their uniforms unbuttoned and their semi automatic rifles lying on the ground beside them. Despite their shabby appearance ,Tim knew that to keep running, after someone had just been shot on the quayside, was to invite them to kill him just to be on the safe side.

He stopped and raised his hands. He was feeling desperate as he saw the car with his new wife continue to drive away. The soldiers were totally confused and clearly leaderless. It was a standoff. Tim looked at them with their guns pointed. They looked at Andrei's corpse and then looked at Tim. Nobody moved for a split second.

The roar of a motorcycle broke the silence. It screeched to halt next to Tim. "Get on," shouted Annubis

Tim had no idea what was happening, but he knew that this was his only hope of saving Jackie. He did not hesitate.

The bike, with Tim on the back and Annubis driving, raced after the Mercedes. The Egyptian security force just stood there and watched in total confusion as they disappeared up the street. One soldier raised his weapon to fire after the departing motorcycle but was quickly ordered not to fire for fear of killing one of the many tourists milling around the quay.

Chapter 20

The motorcycle roared through downtown Luxor with Tim clinging onto Annubis' back. The pedestrians were forced to jump clear as they raced after the departing Mercedes. The car had a big start on the pursuers and in the dense traffic it was hard to spot. Annubis was heading in the general direction of the highway North, in the hope of intercepting the abductors.

Tim was in total shock and was having problems understanding what had just happened. Who were the men taking his wife and who was this man helping him? The questions could not be answered at this point so he clung on desperately, hoping to see the car with Jackie onboard.

Despite all their efforts it soon became apparent that they had lost the car. Annubis pulled the bike off the road and turned off the engine.

"I am sorry my friend we have lost them," he said removing his helmet.

Tim looked at his rescuer, "You," his surprise was plain to see. The last and only time he had seen this man, he had been his captive in Jason Delonge's London flat.. "What are you doing here?"

"I came to kill you," he said.

"But you didn't?"

"You are the one person I would not kill. You gave me revenge for my brother's death. More than that, you were prepared to take revenge for my brother without even knowing him. "

"Where is my wife and who wants me dead?"

"I have no answers, my friend. I was hired to kill but killed the man who was about to kill you."

"Who hired you?"

"That I never know. All I can say that I have worked for them before and I am sure that they are Russian. That is all I know."

"I don't know what to do." Tim felt drained and slumped down onto the ground and put his head in his hands. He was confused and had no idea what, in fact, was happening. One minute he was the happiest man alive on honeymoon with his new wife, then her parents were shot and she was abducted. It was overwhelming.

"My name is Mem," said Annubis. "It is a name I gave up many years ago when my Mother, Father and all of my family died in Iraq. May I call you Anthony?" Annubis had seen Tim's MI5 ID when he searched his wallet in London that fateful night.

"Tim"

"Tim, I know you to work for the British secret service, you must go to them for help surely? They have the resources you need to find your wife."

Tim knew this contract killer to be right but he did not want to leave Egypt while his wife was still here somewhere. "But my wife is here somewhere?"

"Perhaps, perhaps not, but it is certain she will not remain here. Think they did not want her dead or she would be dead. They wanted her alive, she must have something they want."

Tim thought frantically. The attack in England and Jackie's kidnapping had to be linked, but how? "Why did you want to kill me?"

"I did not want to kill you. I was paid to kill you."

"But why?"

"I think they knew you were with MI5 and had little further information about you. I was not even given your name, just your wife's maiden name and a picture of her they had from face book or some other such place. I think they wanted just to ensure that you would not be around to cause complications."

"I need to find out who these people are and what they want?"

"The answers to those questions I think are in England."

"You're right. Take me to the British Consul."

****

Jackie came round in the back of the car, her head pounding. She started to struggle and scream.

"Please to stop that," said the man sat next to her on the back seat of the Mercedes. "It will do no good and I will be forced to hit you again if you do not stop." He was in his thirties and Arab in origin. Another burly Arab sat on her other side. The car was being driven by a further bodyguard type,

"Why am I here? We have no money?"

"I do not know, but we are not kidnappers seeking a ransom. We have been hired to deliver you to someone, beyond that we know nothing, so please shut the fuck up."

The drive was long and tedious. They stopped in backwater villages and she was given food and allowed to go to the toilet. She lost her sense of direction and the constant tension and fear took its toll. They spoke little and her sense of fear grew as they drove north. The journey seemed endless, until they finally arrived in Alexandria.

None of it made sense to her. Her parents, her abduction was spinning in her head. What could these people want with her? Perhaps it was something to do with Tim? Again that made no sense. It was all just madness.

They pulled into what appeared to be an industrial or warehouse complex close to the port area. They entered through gates into a compound that was surrounded by a high wire fence. She was taken from the car and into a warehouse. It was deserted.

"What is happening?" she asked

"We wait."

"For what?" she felt her fear levels rising.

"We wait."

They waited for darkness to fall. During this time bribes were paid to customs and immigration officials by her abductors in order to aid the next phase.

Jackie had fallen into a sleep sat in the chair in the middle of the empty, dusty industrial building when the sound of helicopter blades brought her to consciousness with a start.

"Move"

She was dragged to her feet and into the compound. She was pushed forward to the waiting helicopter. "Head down," said her captors and pushed her into a crouch as they got closer to the rotor blades.

In that moment she took the opportunity to break free and run. She had no idea where she was running to, but she ran. Her captors ran after her and it soon became apparent that there was. in fact, nowhere for her to run. The entire area was secured by a three metre high fence. It was almost with weariness that her captors dragged her back to the waiting helicopter.

Her kidnappers remained behind as the helicopter took off. They were glad she was gone and pleased with their pay-packet for a job well done. She had acquired a new gaoler. A well dressed Russian in his late forties, in a smartly tailored suit. He introduced himself as Igor. She knew that was probably not his name but it made communication simpler to have names, she assumed.

The helicopter headed out into the Mediterranean. Save for the Moon and the navigation lights, it was dark and hard to tell where the sea ended and the night sky started.

"Relax," recommended Igor.

The journey took nearly an hour, until she saw the boat below. The sea was not as calm as it could have been and the pilot was very cautious as he attempted to land on the Yacht's helipad. After a great deal of hovering and arm waving from the crew it eventually settled on the deck. Jackie was firmly taken by the arm and led into the boat and along some corridors to the stateroom.

The door opened and she was greeted by grey haired man with a Russian accent.

"Welcome aboard the Lady Heloise."

Chapter 21

Tim had left the airport and made his way directly to Watford General Hospital. Getting back had proved less difficult than he had imagined. He had managed to contact Stiles who was already aware of Jackie's kidnapping. The British Embassy worked with the Egyptians to get him a flight to Cairo then onward to the UK.

He found his way to Intensive Care and was shown into the room occupied by John. As he entered he saw that Anne and Daniel were sat at his bedside. He was clearly unconscious, had tubes and wires attached to every part of him

Anne looked up," My daughter?"

"I don't know," he said. "She was snatched on the quayside. I have no idea where she is."

"John, has he been shot?"

"Stroke, they fired at him but the bullet missed. We have to wait and see what the damage is." Tears were in her eyes.

Daniel had risen from his seat. "I want Mummy." There were tears in his eyes as well.

Tim put his arms around him. "Mummy will be fine, I promise."

Anne's arm was heavily bandaged and plastered. It was dubious if she would ever regain full use of her arm where the bullet had smashed into the bone and tissue. Only time would tell.

"What is going on?" she asked

"I honestly do not know. There is a Russian connection that is all we can say at the moment."

"What can it have to do with Jackie?"

"Trust me the whole of MI5 is looking at this but so far they can see no connection."

"How long before we know how John is?" he asked.

"It could be hours, day or even weeks. They know there is brain damage to the right side and he will have some paralysis but they can't say at this stage."

Tim looked at Anne and Daniel. It was a sad sight. She was looking very old and frail. Daniel was looking pleadingly at him, with tears in his eyes, to make it all be alright. He felt terrible guilt at their plight as though he should have prevented all this and protected his wife and family.

"It is no good feeling sorry for ourselves, we just have to pick ourselves up and get on with it," said Anne in a forced attempt at positivity. "We need to focus on the here and now. Keep busy and not dwell on things."

Tim knew she was right in a way. He knew there was a reason for all this and he had the resources at his finger tips to sort it out. He knew if there was a connection in all this, GCHQ would piece it together. They were the two dead Romanians, Vadim and Andrei for a start. One in London and one in Luxor. As he sat here talking, MI5 would be tracing all the links, looking for connections. For all intents and purposes, this had been a terrorist attack targeting a MI5 employee and his family. They had the resources and the motivation, but he knew it would take time.

"Listen," she continued, "just before all this happened, John picked up the bottom tier of the Wedding Cake and some table decorations. I thought it a shame to waste them, the ones with the beautiful freesias woven into them. They are still in the boot of our car. He forgot to get them out and they have been there all this time. They will be starting to rot by now."

I'll sort it," he said. "What is happening with Daniel?"

"I get out today and they have organised support for me at home. If I cannot manage I will call you. Don't worry."

"Find Mummy," said Daniel.

"I will trust me," he said. He got up to leave. "I'll be back later."

"Key"

"Oh yes" he said as she handed him the car key.

"You might as well borrow the car and leave it at yours. Neither of us will be driving for a long while yet."

He gave Anne and Daniel a big hug and left the room.

Stiles sat in his car, waiting in the hospital car park, "Alright?"

"Not really I am so worried about Jackie. What is going on?" Tim sat in the passenger seat and Stiles turned on the ignition,

Where to?"

"Jackie's parents', I'll use their car to drive back home."

"We have been working hard at Thames House and we have a good idea who the two Romanians were working for"

"Who?"

"Sokolov Yerik, he is one of those Russian billionaires with links to the Kremlin."

"What the fuck would he want with my wife and family?"

"That we don't know. But you must have done something to him or his cronies. The CIA and MI6 routinely keep tabs on guys like him. The Americans are trying to put the squeeze on the Russians with sanctions, as you know. It is working, Putin is under pressure at home as the economy is grinding to a halt. They are looking at hitting the Oligarchs like Yerik in the pocket by freezing their bank accounts World wide."

"Where is this Yerik now?"

"Not completely sure. He was sighted on his boat moored in Monaco where he met up with two other billionaires, a pair called Lesta and Nikhil. They are all muckers and are all ex what was the KGB. They carved up the Country between them when Communism collapsed."

"I have no knowledge of these people. They are not even my area at the office, as you know. I deal solely with Middle Eastern threats to the UK. It has to be something to do with Jackie but she hasn't any connections to Russia whatsoever. It just makes no sense."

"We'll get there," said Stiles," One thing that is positive, is that they want her alive and have gone through a lot of trouble to keep her that way."

"I just want her home and Daniel wants his Mum back."

The traffic was horrendous as usual and they were crawling along at a snail's pace. It took nearly an hour to travel the few miles from Watford to Pinner.

"Will you be ok?" asked Stiles as Tim got out of the car.

"I'll be fine. I'll drive over to Muswell Hill, sort out the mess from the burglary and clean out the boot of Jackie's Dad's car, then I'll get into the office and try and work out what is going on."

Chapter 22

The two cheetahs looked in fine condition. They walked from one side of their cage to the other following the men, as they walked up and down trying to get a good view of the animals.

"I told you they were in perfect condition," said the vendor

"They do look good. Remind me why you have them for sale?"

Enrique Rojas was about thirty miles from Buenos Aires, the Argentinean capital, on a cattle ranch talking with a man in his early fifties, tanned and clearly used to the outdoor life. The owner of the animals had no idea of who the mysterious buyer of exotic animals was.

"They were destined for a private zoo. They are a breeding pair," he continued. "I used to work in Hollywood providing exotic animals for the movie industry. That was a long time ago now. I could let you see some of the films that have animals I trained in, if you are interested. I supplied the Lions in ..."

"Perhaps later," interrupted Rojas, who had no intention of sitting in the middle of nowhere watching videos with him.

You were saying?"

"Ah yes, the cheetahs, they were destined for a private zoo. I had the usual problems getting the necessary licences and permits but after several months I got the paper work sorted and the beasts into the country,"

"So why are they here?"

"Just the usual in Argentina, the guy who wanted them is in prison, political corruption. So now I am stuffed up with a couple of wild cats."

"So I can take them off your hands for nothing?"

The gaucho laughed," No I couldn't do that, but I would be happy to make my money back and some for the time, trouble and effort involved."

"I do want them but there is the problem of getting them back to my zoo in Mexico," Rojas thought for a moment.

"I can get the export licensee, if you arrange the transport?"

He was clearly eager to get the cats off his hands. Rojas knew that with the right payments bringing the animals into Mexico would not be a problem. He also knew he wanted the cats. He was determined to have the best collection of exotic animals he could for his estate.

The deal was done and he settled into the back seat of the limo for the tedious drive to the Capital. This trip would serve two purposes, the first was the purchase of animals for his zoo, crucially though, it would allow Rojas to escape the attention of the Drugs Lords in Mexico. Since the DEA had been hitting shipment after shipment into the US the suspicion was at fever pitch. Every member of the Cartel suspected the other of being the rat. Rojas had been clever in targeting his and every other dealer apart from his major rival, Oscar Perez Rodriquez.

Rodriquez was not a stupid man and strongly suspected that Rojas was setting him up and targeting his share of the trade. He had been watching Rojas' every move and any hint of suspicious behaviour would have attracted the attention of the other members of the Cartel. Rodriquez would have ensured that.

All the drug lords knew of Rojas' obsession with his private zoo and his desire to be more famous than Escobar and his zoo. They were not surprised at his trip to Argentina to buy some animals. Of course life would be easier if he could just go north to the US and buy animals. In some states individuals had kept bears, snakes and even Tigers in their homes but he liked to see the animals he was buying and travel to the States was fraught with danger. His presence may have been too good an opportunity for US law enforcement to pass up and he could well have found himself the wrong side of a prison wall.

Travel in Latin America was far less dangerous to his freedom, so it was not unusual for him to travel there looking for the stock for his growing menagerie. Free from the prying eyes of the other drug lords, he settled back in the car for the drive to Buenos Aires. There were two further men in the car with him as well as the driver, his bodyguards who watched over his every move.

The old part of the Capital was impressive and had an almost Parisian feel with the Haussmann architecture copied at the turn of the previous century. The traffic blocking the wide Boulevards was, on the other hand not, at all impressive. Eventually they arrived at the thoroughly modern and expensive shopping area. Rojas and his two guards stepped out of the car. They walked past the designer shops in the pedestrian section until they reached the intersection where the restaurant was situated, where Rojas next appointment waited on him

Trist was sat at a table on the pavement under a Sun canopy in front of the steak house. He rose as Rojas approached and extended his hand. The two guards took up position on either side of the table and remained vigilant. "Pleased to see you again," they shook hands and both sat down.

"The steaks are amazing in this country even better than prime US," said Trist as they ordered the flame grilled beef.

"Truly wonderful," agreed Rojas "but we have not come all this way to talk about the cuisine. Have we?"

Trist nodded his head. "The DEA are very happy with the information you have provided."

"Let me guess, now that they have had what they can get from me, they would like to sever their links permanently to save any potential future embarrassment?"

"More or less,"

"No more, no less, they want me conveniently dead. We knew this would be the outcome but did you mange to get me the murderer of my Father?"

"I have done better, I have managed to put myself in the position of being the one to control and organise the whole affair."

"That is indeed very good Mr Trist. Now tell me what the DEA expect to happen?"

"They expect me to engineer your demise using Annubis. I am to convince you that he is here to assassinate your rival Rodriquez, while in fact you will be his target."

"But you will in fact commission him to kill Rodriguez"

"Correct"

"But how can I be sure that you will not double cross me?"

"One, you presumably will not pay me the five millions dollars that would facilitate a comfortable early retirement for me and two I shall personally deliver this Annubis to you."

Rojas looked surprised. "How will you do this?"

"It will be a double hit. The plan is fairly simple. You will call a meeting of the Cartel at your hacienda at which Rodriguez will be present. Annubis will be charged with killing Rodriguez and I shall ostensibly be your assassin. When he has killed Rodriguez I will not kill you but turn my weapon on him and disarm him and if possible deliver him to you alive."

Rojas finished his steak and smiled with satisfaction, both at the quality of the food and with the thought of avenging his Father's death. "Walk with me? I think if you can get this piece of shit that murdered my Father into my hands alive you will be pleased with how generous I can be. Let's say another five million if you do what you say."

Trist smiled and nodded his thanks.

"We are being followed," said Trist

"The young man in shorts and trainers in front of us and the two older thugs behind," said Rojas.

"Yes"

"They intend to mug us," said Rojas. "It is common they snatch bags in this area or relieve people of the possessions at knife point in the richer areas."

"The boy in front, seeing that there were few bystanders, turned and doubled back towards Rojas and Trist, drawing a knife. His two friends closed up from behind and also pulled knives intending to surround Trist and Rojas."

Rojas body guards who had been fully aware of the mugger's attention came up from behind the two muggers, moving in from the rear. They did not see it coming, Rojas bodyguards stabbed both the muggers and lowered them gently onto the side walk and continued walking. As the younger mugger approached from the front he never saw the knife Rojas held. He slumped to his knees, a surprised look on his face as he died.

They walk on as though nothing had happened. Trist knew at that point that he had better keep the right side of Rojas. He was a very dangerous man who enjoyed the hands on approach to murder. There had been no need to kill the muggers, the guards could have revealed their presence and the potential assailants would have faded away looking for a softer target. Rojas had enjoyed the killing and that was the type of creature he was.

Chapter 23

Yerik sat in the stateroom of his Yacht waiting for Jackie to be brought up from her cabin. He was in a reflective mood and his mind wandered back to the past. It seemed an odd set of circumstances that had brought him to this point in life.

He had attended university and looked for a career and more by chance than design had ended up working in the security service. He had been sent to the Andropov Red Banner Institute in Moscow for training by the KGB. The school had been renamed after the famous head of the organisation. They had been trained in their craft and there, he had meet Nikhil and Lesta.

They most strenuous part of the training was to be proficient in foreign languages. He had been fortunate in that his Degree had been in English and German. He had a natural ability for languages. Apart from lectures on the State and Communism, which were incessantly preached at them, they were taught their spy craft. The final part of their course and the most exciting was a three day exercise in Moscow simulating running a field agent. They had all passed and were posted to various countries. He had been sent to England.

Of course, many changes had happened to his home land since those days, the most dramatic being the break up of the USSR. The break up, the social and political upheaval had of course presented opportunities for him and his friends with whom he had stayed in contact.

Now they were rich beyond anything they could imagine. It had not come without a price. Russia was intrinsically corrupt and to stay near the top of the pile you could not be bounded by any form of moral constraint. Yerik did wonder how he had reached a point where he would snatch an innocent woman from her honeymoon and order the death of her husband without a second thought. It was a long way from the idealistic vision he had once held of protecting his beloved Russia.

They had questioned Jackie about the documents and he had considered some form of torture but he knew from his years of experience when some one was lying. It was obvious she did not have a clue what he was taking about.

The documents were somewhere and needed to be recovered. Firstly, to avoid embarrassment, proof of corruption that led all the way to the Kremlin. That would be a propaganda coup for the Americans. Secondly to avoid the loss of their ill-gotten gains, should the Americans decide to extend the sanctions to blocking individual bank account..

In one way, that this woman's husband had not been assassinated as planned when she was abducted might be a blessing. Lee had posted the incriminating documents to her, it was just a matter of locating them. The key would be this woman's husband. Somehow he needed to make contact with him and get him to find the documents and hand them over in exchange for his wife. Yerik's fear was that Tim would find the documents and turn them into MI5. That had to be prevented.

Jackie entered the room accompanied by her gaoler.

"Good evening," he said, as though this was just a normal social encounter and she had not been forcibly taken from Egypt to a boat in the middle of the Mediterranean.

She sat at the table where he indicated. "I should like to have a little discussion over diner, if that is alright with you?"

"Do I have a choice?"

The waiter came in and poured the wine and the starter of smoked salmon soon followed. The quality of the food did little to make Jackie feel any happier.

"What has happened to my son and my parents?" she demanded.

"I assure you they are fine."

She did not know if to believe him or not. In any event she had no choice in the matter, "My husband?"

"He to his well and fighting fit, as they say." "Is the food to your liking?"

She ignored the question, "Why are you keeping me here?"

"That, I am afraid is my dilemma. I was under the impression that you were in possession of some documents that could cause great harm to my friends and me. We did initially hope to force a trade by abducting your son. That did not go as planned. We searched your home for these papers and could not find them so we abducted you in the belief that you would tell us where you stored them. It now seems you have no idea of the location of said papers. Now I am stuck with you and no documents. You see my problem?"

"You could just put me ashore."

"Or I could just dump you overboard. Neither option gets me what I want though."

Jackie felt the fear rise, she knew this man had no real humanity and would dispose of her in the same way most people would throw out an old pair of shoes. "I do not know where these documents are. There is nothing I can do to help you."

The main course had been served and the aroma of duck filled the room. She did not feel hungry and ignored the plate in front of her. Her stomach was cramped in a tight ball as the fear of this monster, sat across the dining table, engulfed her. She felt like screaming, running or throwing herself at his feet weeping for mercy and her life. She knew in her heart that he would not be moved one jot by any of those actions. So she sat still waiting for him to continue.

"If you want to live, you need to work with me."

"I have nothing to offer," she replied simply.

"But you do, your husband."

"My husband, he knows no more than I."

"I accept at this point in time that that may be the case. When the papers turn up I need him to bring them to me and not give them to MI5 or the Americans. You will contact him and get him to cooperate with us. You will have to persuade him."

She felt a moment of defiance and rebelled at his bullying for an instant, "If I don't?"

"I shall kill you, your husband and your son and anyone else that gets in my way for that matter."

She knew he was serious and felt tears come to her eyes. She fought them back in order to keep a small part of her dignity. She sat silently looking down at her plate of untouched food.

"Eat up, there is little point in starving to death," he said, as she poked the food round her plate. "We will set up an untraceable phone link and you will phone your husband and tell him what is required. Do you understand?"

Chapter 24

Tim sat at the dining table at his and Jackie's house in Muswell Hill with his head resting in his hands. He had not moved for nearly an hour. The coffee, he had made earlier, remained untouched on the table before him. He felt helpless.

He had been in contact with the Egyptian police and that had been a complete waste of time. They had been more interested in trying to pin the death of the Romanian on him than trace his wife. Tim knew in any event that Jackie was no longer in Egypt. What he did not know was what her abductors wanted with his wife. The house was in a mess. He did not have the motivation to clean and tidy up. It seemed pointless. So he sat in silence brooding on the situation.

He had gone into Thames House, the headquarters of MI5. His colleagues had been supportive and conciliatory. Of course that was no consolation, the conversation with Elaine, the Director of MI5, offered some hope however.

"I have five people chasing down every bit of Intel on these people and Stiles is heading up the team. We have GCHQ monitoring all traffic and an almost direct feed of the data to the team here. If anything pertaining to your wife, any scrap, any detail comes through, it will be picked up."

Tim was grateful. It was well beyond MI5's area of operations to investigate kidnappings abroad but, given he was an MI5 employee, it could be justified as defending an attack on the Service. He knew Elaine and Stiles would give it their total commitment.

Despite everyone's best efforts, the link between Jackie and the Russians remained illusive. First the attempted kidnap of Daniel and now her abduction clearly showed that the Russians were desperate. Tim had not mentioned that he had been the target of an assassination attempt by the Russians, had he it would have meant exposure of his connection to Annubis. That would have raised difficult questions as to his involvement in Jason Delonge's death and that was a distraction he wanted to avoid at this juncture.

Had this been a normal kidnap and ransom he would have expected contact and demands by now. He would have been assigned an expert negotiating team to deal with the kidnapper's demands. This clearly was not a kidnap for monetary gain. The Russians were among the richest people on the Planet.

He finally roused himself into life when he needed the toilet. He walked through the glass door to the lobby and into the downstairs lavatory. Having relieved himself he walked back into the combined living, dining area and realised what a mess it was. He had not even bothered to unpack the suitcases that had been retrieved from Egypt and forwarded on by the airline.

With a sigh he set to work. The fact he was doing something, even if it was only putting cloths away, hoovering and starting the washing made him feel a little more positive. "Oh shit," he said out loud.

He had just remembered the wedding cake and flowers in the boot of John's, Jackie's dad's, car. He knew that it would not be a pleasant sight and by now the flowers would be festering. He wedged the front door open with a shoe from a pair he had abandoned in the lobby and walked down the path to the car.

He looked at the large brown envelope he had found in the boot. He placed it on the dining table while he had went back to the car with a disinfectant spray and a cloth in an attempt to get the stench from the rotting table displays, which had been in the boot for the last eight or nine days, to dissipate. He was partially successful but the odour still lingered and had permeated the bottom tier of the wedding cake. He put the cake and the dead table displays in a black plastic sack and then put it all in the wheelie bin outside. That left the envelope sitting on the table.

For some reason he felt a sense of reluctance to open it. He had the sort of felling one might have if a private detective had been employed to gain evidence of a cheating spouse. He desperately wanted to know what was in the envelope, posted from Iceland, in the hope it may help him get Jackie back, on the other hand he feared that its contents may be benign and he would not further the return of his bride.

He went to the drawer where he knew there was a box of latex gloves. Jackie had purchased a pack when she saw them on offer at the chemists. She had used several pairs when they had been making up the little gifts, as place markers for the Wedding guests. Jackie had her nails done professionally for the Wedding. She rarely had them painted and really wanted to protect them for the big day. The gloves had seemed an ideal solution. In fact they had been more trouble than they were worth.

Tim struggled to don the gloves but eventually succeed. He did not know the contents, but he did not want to contaminate the papers inside. Any piece of evidence from a finger print to saliva containing DNA could be crucial to the safe return of his wife. He carefully opened the envelope causing as little damage as possible.

With the Icelandic postmark he had already surmised that the letter must be from her dead friend and ex colleague Maurice Lee. He feared that it may contain no more than a badly wrapped wedding gift, such as a book. He was wrong.

He spread the original documents out on the dining table. He knew instantly he had his link to the Russians and why they desperately wanted the contents back. Although he did not understand fully the complexities it was easy to see the billions of dollars and the participants involved. Fear gripped as he realised that this went right to the front door of the Kremlin.

In a sense, knowing what was behind it all was worse than not knowing as the enormity of the forces ranged against him became apparent. The stakes were so high that he and Jackie we mere flies that needed to be swatted.

Tim slumped back in the chair and rubbed his eyes. He felt the tension in his neck and shoulders and the fear in the pit of his stomach, "We're fucked," he said out loud, "completely fucked."

Whatever he did he could see a bad outcome for Jackie. He knew realistically he had no chance of negotiating her release on his own. However he turned the problem in his mind, he could not see himself walking up to the Russians with the documents and them saying thank you and handing his wife back. They would simply kill them both and in doing so completely mop up all the loose ends.

If he showed the documents to Elaine she would immediately hand them to MI6 for onward transmission to the Americans who would instantly go after the money, freeze it, if they could, and have the option to cause major embarrassment to the Russians, when and if they chose to do so. Jackie would just be a tiny piece of collateral damage, not even given a second thought in the high stakes game of international diplomacy.

The only card he had was that Yerik and his merry band of crooks and politicians had no idea where the evidence was. As long as that was the case they would keep Jackie alive as a bargaining chip. That situation would not continue indefinitely and ultimately, Tim would have to reveal he had the goods. Tim knew at that point he was in danger of them just turning up and torturing him, until he gave up the envelope. At that point both he and Jackie would be disposable.

Tim sat silently looking at the ceiling as though divine inspiration would appear from above. A shaft of light shon through the gap in the curtains in front of the french windows that led to the small rear garden. The dust particles rose and fell making intricate patterns, like swirling rainbows in the mist. It reminded him of the hours after his friend Yosuf had been shot and he had been alone and confused, sat in a hotel room not knowing where to turn.

He suddenly remembered the large amount of money and credit cards he had stashed. He realised he was not completely without resources and decided that he should at least retrieve it from the depository as a fighting fund. He made the trip and he was back several hours later with the cash. He had at least the money to fund his fight for his and Jackie's life. Now he needed more.

He would need help. He had one ally in Mem, Annubis, a man who killed for money, a man that had been driven by revenge for years. He knew how to contact him. He had imparted that before they split in Egypt.

Things, if small, were mounting in his favour, money and a contract killer. He also had the resources and intelligence gathering capabilities of MI5 working for him. He knew that realistically he needed more.

The burning question was would Stiles help him to save his wife. He knew that Elaine could not, but Stiles might. As deputy director of MI5 he had a great deal of autonomy. Tim knew he needed his help but how far would their friendship stretch?

Chapter 25

Terrance Mailer's fortunes had a major reversal for the good. Following his interference in MI6's operation in an attempt to aid his long time friend Jason Delonge, he had been demoted to the Back Benches. The change of leadership and a new Prime Minister had seen all that forgotten. He had managed the new PM's leadership campaign and his reward had been the post of Foreign Secretary. Along with that came the oversight of MI6. MI5 of course came under the Home Office.

The first thing he did was to engineer the retirement of the current head of MI6 and his replacement by his inside man Bernard Waverly. He had been part of their old school clique, the people that Mailer considered the "right sort" of people to govern the Country.

Mailer had been shocked at the murder of Delonge but it was all to the good for him. His sordid secrets hopefully had died the night Delonge died. Now of course he was in a position to ensure that his indiscretions with young boys stayed buried. He now had his eye firmly on the PM's job.

He noted that he had a meeting scheduled for later that day with both Bernard Waverly and Elaine Wilkins. Clearly MI5 wanted something but he had no intention of helping the bitch who had help cost him his job. "She could go fuck herself," he smiled to himself.

At Thames house, the headquarters of MI5, there was a meeting in progress. Elaine, Stiles and Tim were gathered in the conference room. Tim had heard nothing as yet from his wife and had kept the existence of the file incriminating Yerik and his cronies to himself. He had not been idle though and had used his time digging out every possible connection and every scrap of information he could, using the full intelligence gathering capability at MI5's disposal. He had set no boundaries to his investigation and had misused his position to delve into every nook and cranny, searching for any scrap of information, scandal or indiscretion that he could conceivably use to help his wife.

"I cannot see what help you expect to receive from MI6," said Elaine," Waverly hates my guts and wouldn't cross the road to piss on me if I were on fire."

"I have to try everything. She is my wife and we know that Yerik has her. However and wherever I get the chance to rescue her I will need manpower. There is no way Yerik is going to turn up with her in mainland Britain, so I need MI6 to help get her back from outside the UK," said Tim.

"What's in it for Mailer? Why would he stick his neck out just to get back a kidnapped woman?" said Stiles. "You have to be realistic."

"Stiles is right. This is really a police matter and not a national security matter," she said.

"I intend to make it a national security matter."

Elaine raised her eyebrows and looked at Stiles in a concerned manner. "Tim you cannot really expect me to be party to some deception that would drag British security into a potential conflict with the Russians. I feel for your dilemma and I would obviously do anything to help as a friend but I cannot misuse my position. You know that."

"I wouldn't ask you to," said Tim "all I have asked is that you get me in front of the Foreign Secretary and I'll take it from there."

"I need to know what you're going to do or say."

"Trust me you don't want to know," said Tim.

Chapter 26

Terrace Mailer had agreed to see them at his Office in the Palace of Westminster, claiming that he had limited time and was due to make a statement to the House on immigration. Elaine, Stiles, Waverly, Mailer and his aide found themselves gathered around the table in the Minister's office.

"As you know I have a very tight schedule today so I would ask that we keep this brief and get to the heart of the matter," said the Foreign Secretary.

Waverly, head of MI6, opened, "This is an MI5 matter and I understand that they are seeking MI6 co-operation in, potentially, a very delicate situation." It was very clear from his body language that he did not want to help in anyway. In fact he held quite a large dislike for Elaine and would have much preferred the head of MI5 to have been one of his old school cronies. She, being a woman to his mind, made it all the more difficult to do business. It was much easier when you dealt with the right sort of people and the right sort of people to his mind were the people that had gone to the same school as he and Mailer.

"What exactly are you asking me to sanction?" said Mailer.

"As you are aware Tim's wife has been taken hostage by a group of Russians. It is not clear what they want at this stage but it is clearly an attack on MI5. It is an act of terrorism against this Country, but outside its borders so we are asking for the resources to combat the threat," said Elaine.

"What is this threat? What do they want?" said Waverly.

"We are unclear at the present," said Elaine. She was telling the truth. Tim had no intention of handing the documents incriminating, Nikhil, Yerik and Lesta over to anyone as they were his only bargaining chip in getting his wife back alive.

"Exactly my point, you are asking for a blank cheque," said Waverly.

"I obviously sympathise with Tim and I would move heaven and earth if it were my wife in this situation but I have to ask, is it in the National Interest, before I authorise intervention in an overseas territory," Mailer said.

"Are you seriously trying to say you will let a bunch of what are after all thugs and thieves hold this Countries Security Service to ransom and sit there and do nothing about it? What sort of message will that send out? Feel free to abduct and blackmail us and will just roll over and take it up the arse," said Elaine.

"I was not suggesting that we roll over and as you so colourfully put it, take it up the arse. I was suggesting we adopt a measured response and await further developments," said Waverly.

"No, you are saying fuck you. It's your problem and I will do my damn best to let you stew," said Elaine.

"Let's just take the heat out of this for a moment," said Mailer. "This bickering will get us no further."

"Look, these bastards have taken my colleague's wife hostage and aim to blackmail us. I need the resources to send out a message to the Russians that they can't fuck with us without consequences," she said.

"Do you have any idea what they are after?" said Mailer.

"Well it will be to do with the money they have stolen to make themselves and their cronies' billionaires. That is for sure. They have no shame, they just take the piss. There is a cellist that is worth millions in theory. In practice the Kremlin have blatantly used him to launder money stolen from the Russian coffers. It would be laughable if it wasn't so serious. They are running rings around the US sanctions. What second rate musician makes millions strumming a fiddle, for Christ sake?" she said.

"In short you haven't got to the bottom of it yet," said Waverly smugly.

"What exactly are you asking for?" said Mailer.

"We suspect that she is being held aboard a yacht in the Med. If we designated it as a terrorist hostage situation it could come to the point where we could use a specialist tactical force to free Mrs Burr."

"You want a navel vessel and the special Boat Service on standby?" asked Waverly.

"Why the fuck not," said Elaine heatedly, "how the hell else are we to get on board a bloody great yacht and rescue Tim's wife otherwise?"

"This all seems a bit too personal," said Mailer.

"Of course it is personal," Tim finally spoke. "She is my wife."

"I understand," said Mailer sounding exceedingly contrite. "But I have to look at the wider implications as Foreign Secretary. Surely you can see that?"

"What I can see is that you are quite happy for these fuckers to get away with it so we can stay friends with the Kremlin," said Elaine.

"I really don't think this is going anywhere. I agree with Waverly we should keep a watching brief at this stage," said Mailer.

"I have a piece of evidence which I think you should consider before you make your final decision," said Tim. He placed a file on the desk in front of Mailer. "For your eyes only, no one else, not even my colleagues at MI5 have seen its contents."

There was silence as Mailer opened the file and began to read. From the expression on his face it was clear that the contents were startling. His expression changed from smug confidence to one of indecision and uncertainty. Closer inspection of his body language would have actually indicated fear.

He looked up from reading the file and he glowered at Tim. There was a brief flash of hatred that he masked almost instantaneously. "I see this information does shed further light on the matter. I thank you Tim for bringing this to my attention. I agree that this information should be held by me alone at this juncture. I assume this is the only copy?"

"There are and there will not be any other copies ever," said Tim. "I shall of course never reveal its contents without your say or the PM's express instruction."

"What is it?" asked Waverly.

"A very delicate matter that needs to carefully considered and is certainly not appropriate to this time and place. It does however change my view on the threat level posed by this situation."

"I have my navel force?" said Elaine puzzled at the turn around.

"To be precise, Tim has his navel force as I would recommend to you that you allow him to head up the operation," he said.

Waverly started to protest but Mailer raised his hand. He stopped protesting. "Now if that is all I declare the meeting closed. I will get my staff to liaise with the Admiralty to get them to come on board, so to speak."

They all left with the exception of Waverly. "I don't understand?"

"That little fuck Burr has somehow got hold of The John Reese Home. Do you fancy reading about that in your morning papers."

Chapter 27

The file Tim handed to Mailer had been the result of a lot of detective work on Tim's part. When he opened the letter from Maurice Lee and saw the names of the men ranged against him he knew this was not something he could deal with on his own. The only ace he had was the evidence against these men and he needed to keep that to himself. There was no doubt that the British and Americans would love to have the dirt on the Kremlin and some of the richest men in Russia, but there was also little doubt that they would do little or nothing to save Tim's wife. She would just be collateral damage. If and when he revealed the evidence, he knew that Jackie would serve no further purpose and would be disposed of. His only hope was to keep control of the file and somehow get the British Government to lend him a hand.

There was absolutely no reason whatsoever for the British to get involved in what on the face of it was the kidnapping of a tourist in Egypt, even if she was married to someone in MI5. Tim knew that he would have to give them the reason and incentive to give him the military back up he might need in getting Jackie back.

He had sat at his desk in Thames House and let his mind go over the events of the last few months. The question that troubled him most was why Waverly had circumnavigated the then head of MI6 and aided Turkish intelligence in their efforts to kill him. Mailer, then a junior minister in the foreign office, had asked Waverly to do it. He knew that Mailer and Delonge were friends, but surely Mailer would not have risked his career on friendship alone? After all he had lost his job at the Foreign Office and would now still be on the back benches had there not been the change in Party leadership and a new PM. His appointment as Foreign Secretary had surprised everyone and then Waverly had benefited by getting the top slot at MI6.

Tim set himself the task of answering the question of why Mailer would risk his political career for Delonge. He set about using all the resources available to him at Thames House and those resources were considerable. There was one hurdle. Mailer was a major politician and there were now strict protocols in place aimed at preventing the use of the Civil Service to spy on and dig up dirt on politicians. These were put in place after a serving British Prime Minister, Harold Wilson, had been the victim of a rogue element in MI5. The CIA thought that Wilson was a Soviet agent and that the KGB had poisoned the previous labour leader, Hugh Gaitskell, to replace him with Wilson. MI5 had illegally burgled homes, tapped phones and spread rumours aimed at destabilising the Government.

Tim needed to circumnavigate the restrictions to allow him free reign to dig into every part of Mailer's life. It did not take him long to cobble together unconnected and unsubstantiated reports on ISIS activity to construct a file, that on the face of it, made Mailer a hot candidate for an assassination attempt. He knew that the whole scenario would not stand any in depth scrutiny, but as it was his job to do the scrutiny, there was little chance of that being a problem.

Tim took his dubious evidence to Stiles, in his capacity as second in command at MI5. "I thought I would throw myself into some work while I wait for news on Jackie. I was just sat at home brooding. So I thought to do something and keep my mind off it."

"You don't have to be here. You know that, don't you?"

"I know but I need to do something and I think I am onto something. There seems to be murmurings of an ISIS attack on the Foreign Secretary."

Stiles was surprised, "Are you sure?"

"Well you cannot ever be one hundred percent sure in this business. It is piecing bits and pieces together and correlation and guesswork. You know that. I do need to dig further into Mailer's lifestyle and background to see where, when and if he is vulnerable. Then make recommendations to enhance the security around him. Of course being in the Government I need express permission to do that."

"Well you have it of course. The last thing we need is to fuck up on a Minister's security, better safe than sorry. Hey?"

"Exactly," said Tim as he left with the authority to put Mailer under the microscope.

Tim was scrupulously methodical and he was good at this part of the job. He delved into every nook and cranny of Mailer's life and looked for links to Delonge, anything that tied them together other than the usual school, university and professional relationships that would be expected.

Tim was getting to feel frustrated. He knew Delonge had been a paedophile and a child murderer. He also knew that Mailer had been prepared to let Waverly sell Tim down the river to the Turks, so there had to be something.

The Rubicon Club popped out at him. They both were members. He knew that the Rubicon was the river boundary that Caesar had crossed when his army entered Rome to take control in forty one BC but that was not a great deal of help. The Oxbridge way was always to give mediocre things grandiose classical names. The internet gave him the answer, a canoeing club.

They had both been members of a canoeing club. That was not that promising. There was little hope of that fact yielding anything to induce Mailer to lend support to Tim and his wife. He was beginning to despair. Was he wasting his time?

He soldiered on. He got everything he could on the Rubicon Club using the full resources available from GCHQ in his quest. He was flooded with insignificant details, member's lists, club accounts, competition results and expeditions. The Club seemed perfectly normal in everyway. It even ran courses to encourage the young and up and coming to join the sport.

Tim sat back and rubbed his eyes. Then he saw something that stimulated his interest. The Club ran away trips for young boys aged between eight and eleven. The boys were all at one particular care home "The John Reese Home." The Rubicon would take six boys on field trips for a few days. The boys were in care and came from dysfunctional homes and had often been subjected to abuse.

Tim was now no longer feeling despondent as he delved further. Mailer and Delonge had frequently taken these young boys canoeing and on camping trips. He knew of Delonge's interest in small boys and he now suspected that Mailer had shared his proclivities. That they took boys on field trips was of course no proof that Mailer had been involved in anything untoward, but he knew he had to follow the only link he had.

Police reports came in and there had been allegations made but there had been the usual reluctance to follow the matter further. Small boys do not make good witnesses and Tim could see that the police had been less than enthusiastic in investigating the complaints. Now, many years later the police were being forced to investigate claims of historic child abuse owing to victim and public pressure. The John Reese Home however, was not to be investigated.

It was going to be investigated now though and Tim set about doing it. He soon had a list of kids that had been taken out of the School by Mailer and Delonge and the dates. Tim was using MI5 resources without stint. He put in request after request and kept digging. He had everything from weather reports, road traffic incidents, in fact anything he could think of that might have happened in the vicinity of the field trips.

His efforts paid off. He had managed to track down five of the boys who had been on the canoeing trips with Mailer and Delonge. He had GCHQ troll tax records, criminal records, council tax records, job centre records, job seekers payments and even local press reports until he had his names and their current whereabouts.

He knew there had to be more but time was against him. He went for the nearest name on the list Kevin White. He worked in the City for City Bank. Tim announced his MI5 credentials and spoke to him. The meeting was arranged and Tim took the tube to St Paul's

"I understand you were in care at the John Reese Home?"

"That was a long tome ago."

"Did you go on the canoeing trips organised by the Rubicon Club."

"Uncle Terry and Uncle Jason's camping trips, I did."

"Can I ask you about them?"

"As I said that was a long time ago. I am a trader now with a major bank. I am not sure what purpose would be served by raking things over."

"You know, of course, that Uncle Terry is Foreign Secretary now?"

"The fact had not escaped me and that is all the more reason why I do not want to get involved."

Tim looked him straight in the eye. "Tell me, you were abused weren't you?"

White was clearly very uncomfortable and looked down. Tim could see the pain and humiliation in him. He answered slowly as if dragging to the surface long discarded thoughts. "I was determined not to let those scumbags fuck up my life. I have made my way and now have a life and I don't want to rake it up. For what it is worth they abused us and what is more the staff did nothing to stop it and some even colluded in the activities. The police were just not interested and any boy that spoke out was terribly punished."

"Would you give me a written statement?"

"I won't and I will deny this conversation if you try and involve me. I have moved on."

Tim went away, knowing that he was right but also knowing he needed more that knowing. He needed evidence. Not the evidence that could be used in court, but enough to use as a lever to get Mailer's support.

The block of flats just outside Hatfield was run down like the rest of the Town Centre. Joe Platt lived here. He had been on Uncle Terry's trips and he had not done as well as White. He was a known drug user and had a criminal record for burglary, theft and handling stolen goods.

It took a great deal of banging on his front door before a bleary eyed girl opened it. Tim saw immediately that she was strung out on some drug or other. "Twenty pounds to fuck me or thirty to do me up the arse." She was naked and the needle marks were clearly visible down her arms.

He gave her thirty pounds and pushed past. She followed him in and the started to bend over the edge of a dirty stained sofa presenting her bottom to him. He ignored her and walked through the door from the living room past a bathroom and into the bedroom. Platt was lying naked on a dirty mattress surrounded by the usual drug taking paraphernalia of syringes, tin foil and a soot stained spoon.

"Wake up," said Tim poking him with his foot.

Platt groaned and Tim pushed him harder. He roused himself and opened his eyes. Tim moved to the curtains and pulled them back letting the light stream in.

"Who the fuck are you?" shouted Platt.

"My name is Burr and I am with MI5," he showed his ID.

latt struggled with the concept and the naked girl stumbled into the room. "Don't you want to fuck me?" she asked confused.

"Get dressed or I'll take you in and let you go cold turkey."

They girl pulled a T shirt on that just about stretched down far enough to cover her genitals and he pulled on a pair of grubby jeans and a stained T shirt.

Platt was sat on the stained sofa and she was boiling a kettle in the kitchen. "I need some information and I need you to give it to me. I have a grand here if you give me the right answers and I have a cell waiting if you don't. Do I make myself clear?"

"As fucking day, what do you want?"

"You were at the John Reese Home?"

"So what?"

"I want you to tell me bout the canoeing trips with Uncle Terry."

"That fucking cunt, what do you want to know?"

"Did he molest you? Did you see him molest others?"

"It wasn't just him. There was that other fucker Uncle Jimmy,"

"Jason not Jimmy."

"That's it Jason. They were dirty fuckers the pair of them. I hate them."

Tim got out the envelope containing the thousand pounds and put it beside Platt. Yosuf's money was about to do some good. "Tell me what happened then you can have the money." The girl staggered in with the coffee.

Tim had planned to take a statement if he could and had A4 paper and a pen. The paper had been double folded in his jacket pocket. It would be scrappy. Tim knew that a deposition obtained like this, with the offer of money would not stand up in Court. It was not intended to but it would be enough to launch a press investigation and force the police to act. Mailer would be fucked in any event and it was only the threat that Tim needed.

Tim wrote and Platt spoke. Platt signed and received the money. Tim had his statement. He included a list of all the boys, the dates and the statement in the file .It had worked and Tim got the back up he needed when he put the file on Mailer's desk.

Chapter 28

"Well, what happened?" asked Stiles as Elaine entered her office at MI5 headquarters in Thames House. She had just returned from her meeting with Mailer, Waverly and Tim.

"Let me get my coat off," she slide open the door to the built in cupboard and pulled out a hanger and carefully arranged her coat on it before placing it back. Stiles could not help but notice the eight or ten pairs of shoes neatly arranged in the bottom of the cupboard.

"Nice shoes," he said.

"Don't take the piss," Elaine Wilkins was always capable of surprising people with her ability to be fouled mouthed. Although she had a PhD in something from some Oxford college she liked to demonstrate her humble origins by retaining the colourful language of her pre educated days. Stiles had learned to interpret the meaning of her sayings. For example, "crap," meant "with all due respect, I feel that could stand further analysis," "Bollocks" meant "you have not considered the wider implications" and "Piss off" meant, "Piss off."

"Are you going to tell me what transpired at the meeting?"

She sat back in her chair. "As expected, Mailer and Waverly were having non of it and were sending us off with a flea in our ear."

"So you were told to piss off, using your language?"

"Until Tim handed a file to Mailer and then all change."

"That must have been nice to watch?"

"It was quite enjoyable, when Mailer looked at the file he almost chocked," she paused. "Now tell me what you have found out. What was in that file, what is Tim up to and why have the Russians taken his wife?"

"Are you sitting comfortably? Then I shall begin. Firstly, our friend the new Home Secretary, Tim came to me with a cock and bull story about an ISIS threat to his life and wanted access to all his data."

"And you granted it?"

"Of course it does no harm to know all the dirt and it is our job to deal with any potential terrorist threat."

"Of course, even if it is imaginary."

"I trust my operatives. If Tim says there is a threat, there is a threat as far as I am concerned. He is the expert in that area and I am bound to take his concerns seriously."

"Of course you are," agreed a smiling Elaine.

"Tim went through Mailer's and Delonge's backgrounds with a fine tooth comb. He settled on a link with a kid's home. Both Delonge and Mailer used to take boys out of the home."

"I get the link. What is wrong with these public school tossers? So Tim dug up some evidence of some historic child abuse and let Mailer know. That explains why he changed his mind and why he got Waverly to intervene to protect Delonge when he was Ambassador. What it doesn't explain is why Waverly helped him? Is he a paedophile?"

"I can't find anything on Waverly but investigating the head of MI6 is not that easy. I am pretty sure he is not and I think it is a matter of mutual back scratching. Waverly covers and helps Mailer and in return it has paid off with his getting the top job at MI6."

"So what else has our Mr Burr been up to?"

"Checking out the Russians and so have I. I think I can, more or less, piece it together."

"Alright, don't milk it, just tell me what is going on."

"The first thing has nothing to do with MI5 or Tim. It has everything to do with his wife."

"She is just some sort of bean counter. Isn't she?"

"It is who she counts beans for. When I was best man at the wedding she was pretty upset that an old friend had just died in Iceland in suspicious circumstances. It was the only odd thing that has happened, so I have put the wheels in motion and had every last thing followed up regarding Mrs Burr and the dead chap Maurice Lee."

"Don't make me think. Just lay it out before me."

"I cannot prove any of it but I think that we have the following situation. Lee works for, or did work for, the Baltic Bank in Iceland. The first thread I had checked out was the Bank. It is owned by a series of other banks and a mishmash of holding companies."

"Let me guess. It is controlled by our Russian mates? Am I right?" said Elaine.

"You are right, "all knowing one." It has possible links right to the doors of the Kremlin."

"So what's their angle?" she asked.

"They have done a ridiculously generous deal with the Iceland Government and Banks to virtually underwrite the release depositors funds locked up in their banking system."

"They are washing their ill gotten gains and avoiding US sanctions?"

"Got it in one," said Stiles.

"What's Mrs Burr to do with all this?"

"Now this is pure conjecture but logical. The firm of auditors she works for just got the biggest audit of their life, the Baltic Bank. A Bank of this size would normally elect one of the top four of five firms of accountants but they have opted for a five partner firm. On the back of it she has made partner. I gave them a ring and basically her connection with the dead bloke, Lee swung the audit their way."

"If we penetrated the ruse that easily, surely the CIA could do the same?" said Elaine.

"They probably have but it is a matter of proof. We cannot prove that the Russians have anything to do with it nor can the US I am guessing. You cannot just go round freezing the assets of banks on a hunch."

"Now it becomes clear. Lee stumbles on the proof and turns to his close friend Jackie for help, after all she is the Baltic Bank's auditor. The Russians get wind of it and dispose of Lee but the proof of their involvement has already been passed on."

"Exactly, they search her house and can't find it. They assume she has it stashed somewhere. An attempt is made to abduct her son to instigate a trade, the boy for the proof. They fuck it up and dead bodies end up lying around the streets of London."

"So they turn to plan B, kill Tim and abduct his wife and get her to reveal the whereabouts of the file."

"That's my guess. One big problem with their master plan, she knows nothing about the file or its whereabouts."

"It turns up after they leave to go on honeymoon, surely not?"

"I think that is what happened. In fact I think I am responsible for setting the whole train of events in motion."

"You are kidding me?"

"No I am not. I forgot the button holes and we dashed out to get them. The postman turned up with a parcel that needed signing for. We were in so much of a rush to get to the Wedding that had to leave a card and took the parcel back to the sorting office."

"Is it still there?"

"Nope, Jackie's Father collected it while she was on Honeymoon."

"Let me guess, Tim has it now?" said Elaine

"That is what I think. He is going to use it to bargain for his wife."

"And he has just blackmailed MI6 to affording him backup," she said.

"Using you words, he is a smart bugger isn't he?" said Stiles.

"Too fucking smart by half, but the question is, what should we do?"

"That, my esteemed leader, I am glad to say, is up to you."

Elaine looked up at the ceiling and let out along sigh. "The right thing to do is detain Tim and get him to hand over the evidence of the money laundering scam, pass the file over to the Home Secretary and let the politicians decide how to use it."

"That would condemn his wife to death," said Stiles.

"That goes with the territory," said Elaine.

"She didn't sign up for that."

"No but we did."

"Is that your decision then?" Stiles knew if she decided on that course of action he would warn Tim and make sure he got clear. He knew that file would never be used by the politicians it would be kept and used as a bargaining chip and Jackie would die for nothing.

"Of course it isn't," said Elaine, "I am not a total fucking arsehole."

She could see the relief on Stiles' face. She also knew that he would have warned Tim and aided him in saving Jackie. At least she would retain control this way, as opposed to having two rogue MI5 agents running amok in a private war.

"Has Tim been contacted by any of the Russians to do a trade?" she asked.

Stiles was not going to say anything and had buried the intercept of Tim's call from Yerik if Elaine had chosen the option of following the book and detaining Tim.

"You were going to keep that titbit from me. Weren't you?"

He just smiled. "He is my friend, she is my friend."

"Well I am the best friend both of you will fucking ever have," said Elaine. "Talk to him. Get him to confirm what we suspect. Then put together a plan to get his wife back."

"What about the file?"

"What file?" she smiled. He nodded and rose to leave, "We never had this conversation, it's your balls on the line, not mine," she said.

Chapter 29

Annubis had always worked on his own and he had grave doubts as to working as part of a team. He sat in his hotel room in Mexico City and avoided the issue in his mind. His life had been one of loneliness and self reliance from war torn Iraq, through the refugee camps and the orphanage there had only been himself he could rely on. When his brother died he knew he stood alone and would give his trust to no one. With this latest assignment he understood that there were multiple targets and that made escaping cleanly difficult. He would not only need to make the hit and have an exit strategy. He would need to ensure he distanced himself from the other shooter.

There were too many unknowns. Firstly, could he trust the man he had to work with? He knew nothing about him nor could he. People in his line of work did not lay out their life achievements on Linkedin.

Then there was the simple problem of ensuring they acted in concert. It would be of little use if they did not acquire their targets simultaneously and fire within an instant of each other. Once the first shot was made there would be a dash for cover and possible counter measures from any bodyguards.

Thirdly, once that first bullet left the barrel their presence and position would be compromised. An ill coordinated attack would give the intended targets' security, just that little longer to respond and mount a counter attack.

The planned location was not at all to his liking. Normally he would stalk his target. Get a feel for him. Check his routine and habits and look for an opportunity to strike. He would have the element of surprise, terrain and location of his choosing. He was being denied these choices on this occasion.

He studied the map for what seemed the thousandth time and could not see a clear exit route. There was to be a gathering of the main players in the drug game at the Hacienda of Enrique Rojas, who was to be assassinated by his fellow hit man. His target was to be Rodriguez.

The location was just not suitable. There was only a single road in and out. The land around the compound and house where the meeting was to be held had little in the way of cover. To add to the mix, the owner had turned it into some sort of wild life park with lions, hippos and god knows what else roaming about.

e would not even consider the contract normally but he had no wish to get on the wrong side of the CIA. They would have no hesitation in putting him out of business permanently and they had the resources to do it. They could have done this job without a problem with the technology available to them. Drones were being used all over the Middle East to target and neutralise ISIS and other terrorist leaders. Of course Mexico was not a terrorist organisation and the CIA wanted to keep its hands clean as far as it could. Annubis realised that the CIA were probably doing the Drug Enforcement Agency a favour in this case, but he still did not want to rock the boat.

As the time came closer for his meeting with his co-assassin, his doubts became worse but he had to put his misgivings behind him. He left the room and headed for the pick up point in the hired jeep.

They drove in silence. They had been in the Jeep for three hours when they pulled into the roadside stop to refuel and grab a bite to eat. Trist had had no need to come up with a cover story or identity. He introduced himself as Dog and as Annubis was the jackal headed god of ancient Egypt, they shared a joke that they were two dogs on a day out.

They sat under an awning at the roadside cantina and ate their tacos, both drank bottled water. Trist spoke first, "I have been given a detailed layout of the estate and aerial photographs."

Their employers had obviously been more forthcoming to Dog than they had been to Annubis. The pack of documents was passed across the table. The first thing Annubis noticed was the amount of construction underway in and around the compound. Rojas was certainly going for the zoo in a big way. Finished buildings and partly constructed ones had pooped up everywhere to house the birds, animals and reptiles that were being acquired from around the World.

Trist spoke, "I think there is adequate cover to conceal us while we wait to take our shots."

Annubis could see the possibilities. Trist had the advantage of Rojas providing him with the plans and then taking those plans to a crack operations planning team at Langley. Trist knew he had the best planned assassination that the CIA could come up with. He counted on this to convince Annubis to go ahead with the hit on the Drug Lord.

The meeting of the Cartel members was in three days and would be in the form of a barbeque. This would afford the assassins the best opportunity to shoot Rodriguez and Rojas. Trist of course had no intention of taking the shot on Rojas, preferring to take the ten million dollar bounty the man had effectively placed on Annubis for the killing of his Father.

"How do we extract ourselves?"

Trist and the Langley planners had wrestled with the problem for ages. Of course they were under the impression that Trist and

Annubis would be pursued vigorously by the Drug lord's foot soldiers. In reality Trist had no such problem. Rodriguez would die and Annubis would be handed to Rojas. Trist would be free to just drive off into the Sunset with no let or hindrance from Rojas's men.

"There is only one feasible way, helicopter."

"Two points, do we have one and secondly, they certainly do have one."

Trist smiled, "We do and they won't."

Annubis was unsure of what to make of the reply and remained silent and allowed Trist to continue.

"The CIA has given me a local contact that they have used in the past, when they or the Mexican Government want deniability of the involvement in semi legal activities. In truth I suspect that it is funded by the CIA. It is a genuine helicopter hire business, on the face of it doing survey work, moving frieght to tricky locations and it has even lifted a cross onto the dome of a church that fell off and had to be put back."

"Go on," said Annubis.

"It will be camouflaged and within three minutes flying time of our location. We of course will not contact it, maintaining radio silence until we have taken the hit. I am pretty sure that these guys monitor the radio channels for police or government activity and the last thing we want to do is forewarn them of our presence."

"I agree but their helicopter," it could clearly be seen on the aerial photographs Annubis had before him.

"That is up to us. We do the hit and fire tracer rounds and everything we can at it to disable it. I am pretty sure I can shoot the tail rotor and damage it from over a mile. Anyway even if it is still serviceable after we take a few pops at it, we will be miles ahead in flying time before they can respond."

Annubis felt that risks were becoming manageable and there was a very good chance of fulfilling the contract and getting out alive. "OK, lets reconnoitre," he said..

Trist suppressed a smile. There was of course no helicopter planned escape. He would be the only one leaving and he had a free pass just to drive out of there.

Chapter 30

After the phone call from Jackie, Tim immediately left Thames House. He knew that the people at MI5 were not stupid and that given time they would make the connections and work out that he obviously had something the Russians wanted. It followed that if they wanted it so did MI5. He was right in his assumption because even as he left the building to get the file and cash from his stash, Stiles was laying out the whole affair to Elaine.

He had no intention of doing the right thing and handing the evidence of money laundering and corruption that laid a trail all the way to the Kremlin. The only thing he wanted was to get his wife and Daniel's Mother back alive. He was not going to allow Jackie to become a pawn in an international game of diplomacy.

He walked up to John and Anne's house in Pinner. He had parked their car outside and would take a taxi to Gatwick airport where his flight was due to depart in six hours time. He rang the door bell and he heard the sound of running.

Daniel opened the door with an expectant and excited look on his face, "Have you found Mummy?"

Tim put his suitcase down in the lobby, picked him up and hugged him. "No not yet, I am just off to get her. I just wanted to say good bye to Grandma and Grandad."

He carried Daniel through to the living room as Anne walked in from the kitchen," I have put the kettle on"

"Tim is just going to fetch Mummy and bring her home," said

Daniel.

Anne looked expectantly at Tim for answers. "I have been contacted by her abductors, they want something Jackie had and I now have. I'm going to meet them and do a trade."

"Will they give her back unharmed?" Her Mother's face was full of concern.

"Of course they will. They have no reason not to," said Tim with more confidence than he felt. "How is John?"

"Making progress, he still can't talk but the physiotherapy is gradually getting him some movement in his left arm. Why don't you pop up and see him while I make the tea?"

He walked up the stairs to the bedroom. John was propped up in bed and Anne had placed the television at the foot of the bed so he could watch it. His eyes moved to the side to watch Tim enter the room. "How are you?"

John could only make a semi gurgling noise in response but from the look in his eyes, Tim knew the only thing he wanted to hear about was his daughter's safety. Tim sat on the edge of the bed. "Don't worry, I shall get her back. I am on my way to do that now. Trust me, I will not let anything happen to her."

He readjusted the pillows and went back downstairs. "How's the arm?"

"Good as new," she said as she brought in a tray with tea and biscuits. Daniel immediately went for the biscuits. "Leave some for me," said Tim.

He phoned for the taxi and spent a tense twenty minutes waiting for its arrival. His mobile phone buzzed as the driver rang to let him know he was outside the property. He got up and went towards the lobby. Daniel ran after him.

"You will bring Mummy back won't you, promise?"

He gave Daniel a hug. "I promise," he said.

He walked down the front path pulling his case behind. The door closed and he saw the taxi parked down the road about fifty yards to his left. He walked towards it.

"You need to come with us Mr Burr," the voice said. Tim had been so absorbed in looking back at the house and thinking of the pain that Daniel was experiencing that he had not noticed the three men get out of the car.

"Special Branch," asked Tim.

"Afraid so," came the reply.

He found himself wedged between the two burly officers on the back seat as they drove off.

"You would think you didn't like us, the way you left without saying goodbye," said Stiles. He was sat in Stile's office with his suitcase by the door next to another case which had already been there on his arrival.

"I like you a lot. I just want to get my wife back," said Tim.

"Where is the file?"

"Just in my bag."

"Good a place as any I suppose. Now tell me the truth, I think we have it all worked out but I would just like conformation as to how clever I am. Maurice Lee, the chap who died before the Wedding, sent Jackie a load of paperwork implicating our Russian fiends in a scam to launder money using the Baltic bank. Am I right?"

"One hundred per cent," said Tim.

"I know you are on your way to trade the papers for Jackie because we are pretty good at surveillance here, some would say that we are one of the best in the World at it. So I just took the precaution of having your phone bugged and monitored."

"I need that file. Please don't take it. It is all I have to get Jackie back alive," Tim was almost pleading with Stiles.

"What file?" said Stiles. Elaine and I don't recall even a mention of a file in any conversation we did not have.

"Why am I here then? "The relief in Tim's voice was clearly recognisable.

"We are going on holiday together." Stiles reached into the drawer in his desk and pulled out three passports. He pushed them across to Tim who picked them up. They were CD passports, Corps Diplomatique, one in his name, one in Jackie's and the third in Stiles'. "Though we might as well make travel as easy as possible and avoid all that tricky customs stuff."

"Thank you," Tim was genuinely touched.

"We will get her back. I have organised the flight and hotels and thanks to your clever but slight dubious negotiations with Mailer, we have backup already on its way just in case our Russian friends were thinking of getting physical."

"Come on let's go and get your beautiful new wife back," he said and headed for the door.

Chapter 31

Stanley Jones looked out across the deck of the HMS Defender, a type 45 destroyer. He was glad to be back in the Med after their posting to the Gulf, where they had been on patrol in an effort to reduce the risk to shipping of a terrorist attack. The heat in the Gulf had played havoc with the ship's engines and their mission had mixed fortunes. In fact Captain Jones' command hung in the balance after a super tanker was successfully attacked by ISIS backed terrorists.

They had been patrolling Libyan waters in an effort to stop and apprehend the people smugglers bringing migrants across the Mediterranean to Europe. In fact the British warship could, in reality, do very little to make a difference on the trade in human misery.

The smugglers have two ways to send their human cargo across the sea. One is the use of inflatable rafts and this is by far the most common method. Loaded to the gills with passengers they set to sea. The smugglers do not man the boats themselves so there is no opportunity to catch them or deter them.

The other way, the human cargo is transported to Europe, is in wooden fishing trawlers. These are bought from local fishermen just before a planned trip, giving authorities little time to respond. Moored out at sea on the night of a smuggling trip where they wait to be filled by the smugglers ferrying the passengers in small inflatable boats. Again they are loaded to capacity before heading for Europe. The smugglers employ low level expandable fishermen to just about keep the boat moving.

Whatever method used, the Navy has little opportunity to make an impact on the trade as there is no chance of catching the people truly profiting, as they never put themselves in reach.

They were entering the harbour at Souda Bay where the United States Naval Support Activity is located. Souda Bay is on the northwest coast of the Greek island of Crete. The Greek Navy also had a large naval base which occupies a large portion of the north and south coast of the harbour. Jones would be hosting a dinner for a few of his fellow naval opposite numbers. He would be waving the flag for Britain.

The orders to divert from their people smuggling mission in Libyan waters to Crete had all been very last minute and was a little surprising. Jones however was even more surprised when he was ordered to facilitate a small team of six Special Boat Service personal in going ashore under cover of darkness. He was also ordered to put the helicopter on standby to provide support for them should it be necessary.

Moored in the harbour of the town was the Lady Heloise. Jones had specific orders to keep her under surveillance at all times. The yacht would appear, may be involved in the human traffic trade, according to intelligence reports. He trained his field glasses on her and felt that if the luxury yacht was involved in smuggling it would be the most unlikely candidate he had even seen in his experience.

Jones was intelligent enough to understand that the smuggling was merely a justification and that he would be unlikely ever to know why a destroyer was shadowing a pleasure boat. Even more puzzling was that his orders also required him to keep ready a fully armed boarding party in readiness, to seize the lady Heloise should he be instructed to do so. Logically, the Cretan coast guard were the people for the job and not a type 45 destroyer. The only thing he brought to the table was that he could blow the yacht to smithereens in an instant and that was even odder in that his orders also made proviso for him to do just that. Jones surmised that whoever was on that yacht had seriously pissed someone off in Whitehall and the Admiralty.

Aboard the Lady Heloise, Jackie was settling down to breakfast with Yerik. "So you see, if your husband keeps to his side of the bargain, this time tomorrow you will be sitting down to breakfast together," he said.

Jackie still had no idea what the whole affair was about. She had been snatched in Egypt, driven to the back and beyond, helicoptered to this boat and sailed around the Med. "Where are we?"

"Crete, it is the largest of the Greek Islands. Why don't you go up on deck and get some sun after breakfast. Rest, as you will be having a late night."

She had no choice and accompanied by her ever present guard, she spent the day sunning on deck. She wanted to believe Yerik that soon she would see Daniel and Tim and this nightmare would be over, but in truth she trusted him not a jot.

She walked to the side of the deck and lent over. The bodyguard was alongside her in an instant. She had contemplated jumping to the sea and attempting to swim for freedom but that option was not to be allowed her. Se could see the HMS Defender across the bay and wished she had some means of getting help.

Jones had his binoculars trained on the deck of the lady Heloise and was watching the attractive bikini clad young woman approach the guard rail. "Not bad, not half bad," he said to himself. "I wouldn't mind rescuing her."

Chapter 32

The Sun was shinning as they arrived at Heraklion airport. Their transit had been easy. They had loaded their entire luggage into the diplomatic pouch. The pouch, in this case, was a large metal box that it took the two of them to carry. The excess baggage charge had not been nice but the airline had been accommodating to the two men from MI5. The Greeks had of course wondered why there was a need for two diplomats to travel to a Greek island, but the cover story of people smuggling from Libya and the possible threat to the EU was sufficient to satisfy their curiosity. The Greek Government were open to any help in stemming the flow of migrants into their Country as they were struggling in funding the cost of the massive influx they had been experiencing over the last few years.

Tim and Stiles found the car rental company just inside the airport terminal. Stiles had managed to secure a jeep with off road capability and satellite navigation installed. The paper work was soon completed and they wheeled their box out of the terminal across the road and into the car rental lot.

After a false start in the wrong direction they were driving along the road with the sea in view. Gloriously blue, the waves lapped the shore and the Sun shone with an intensity not found in England. If it were not for the cloud of Jackie's captivity hanging over them it would have been an idyllic start to any holiday.

They turned off the main highway at a sort of temporary round about with excavators parked up around piles of earth on either side. It was fairly clear that a major road improvement scheme had been started then abandoned as funds ran out with Greece's worsening economic crises. A small road led off towards a mini theme park and play area and a golf course in the distance. The track wound past stoney fields with a mixture of olive trees in which sheep were grazing.

Stiles was driving and passing the tennis courts, he pulled up outside the main building at the Golf Resort Hotel. The hotel was a holiday resort complex with individual apartment blocks laid out across the site linked by pedestrian walkways. The golf course could be seen in the distance while closer to hand were the swimming pools, tennis courts and even a crazy golf course.

"It is very holiday village," said Tim.

"I know but it is all the accommodation we could get at short notice. It will serve its purpose though," said Stiles.

They had two apartments at ground level, their layouts were identical. The external door opened onto a living area with a dining table for four on the right as you entered. Directly ahead was a seating area with two chairs and a sofa bed facing a television. Beyond, through two large opening glass doors, was a terrace with a table and chairs. To the left as you entered was a wide passageway that was fitted as a kitchen, passing the cooker and hob on your left was a door leading to the bathroom. To the right of the bathroom was a large airy bedroom with further glass doors opening onto the terrace.

Tim and Stiles were sat on the terrace at Tim's apartment. The terrace was separated from the pathways and gardens beyond by a low metal fence. There was clearly a problem with stray cats in Crete. As soon as they settled in the chairs on the patio the cats began to wander up and through the gaps in the railings in the fence. They were bold cats and Tim found he had to keep the patio door pulled to, as they would dash into the apartment at every opportunity in a search for food. One lapse in security Tim realised would result in the apartment being marked as the cat's territory with a deposit of cat's urine.

"The plan?" said Stiles.

"The rendezvous is up in the hills behind the port of Chania. It is remote, past a little village. There is one road in and one road out."

"Not good from a strategic point of view. They will have the advantage over our movements. Do you have the map coordinates and time?"

Tim passed him his cell phone. Stiles copied them into his phone and pressed send.

"What was that? I can't have you risking Jackie's safety. I don't give a shit about the file. I will hand it over and get my wife back."

"Insurance, just in case we have problems getting out."

Tim had no choice but to take Stiles at his word but he still feared that the draw of having leverage over the Russians would be too much to expect the UK security forces to pass up without at least an attempt to keep hold of it.

"Lets see what is in our goody box." Stiles opened the diplomatic bag. He handed the file that Maurice Lee had lost his life over to Tim, making a great show of not looking at it. Tim took it without saying a word. At this point in time it was the most precious item in the World for him as it represented his only hope of saving his wife and Daniel's Mother.

Stiles then pulled out two metal boxes, they were oblong and very well made in bright aluminium. He handed one to Tim who unlatched the lid and opened it. There was a gun inside. At first Tim thought it was the Markarov that he had become familiar with when Yosuf and acquired two for them both. It was similar but when he felt it in his hand it was lighter. Stiles smiled, "Just like James Bond a Walther. Do you know how to use it and load it?"

"Yes," said Tim realising that the Markarov had been virtually a copy. Stiles passed him the ammunition and a shoulder holster. Stiles dug further into the large box and pulled out two bullet proof vests.

"Are you planning a fucking war?" said Tim.

"Just put it on and we'll get them adjusted so they hang properly and cover all the right bits, better safe than sorry."

There were further goodies in the box, high powered torches and two large knives. They sorted everything out and laid it out on the bed in the rear room ready for their sojourn later that night.

The day dragged slowly and the tension mounted. If Tim thought about the exchange his stomach felt like there were a small football team having a kick about in it. He tried watching the television but there was only one English Channel and that was showing a rerun of an antiques buying show. Stiles was dealing with matters in an easier fashion. His previous life with the Navy had taught him the art of making the most of down time before an operation. He had a little snooze and ate well when they drove down from the resort and found a local Taverna. In contrast Tim could not relax and had little appetite.

"For crying out load, just relax will you. You are making me nervous and that is not the way we need to be," Said Stiles as Tim got up and paced around his apartment. "Stop worrying we shall get her back safely and you will wake up together here tomorrow morning as though you were still on honeymoon."

"Right," said Tim

"Well, I will let you do a bit more pacing and worrying. I am going to my apartment to get some shut eye so I don't nod off while we are playing swap the hostage tonight. Try and rest it will be a long night."

He left and Tim was on his own. He knew Stiles was deliberately playing the risks down. It was quite possible that they could all be dead in a few hours. He appreciated the risk Stiles was taking on his behalf. MI5 need not be involved in this at all but Elaine had rallied to support him and Stiles was putting himself in physical danger for him. There was little to be done in reducing the risks any further. The biggest factor going for his and Jackie's safety was Stiles. He was the deputy director of MI5. Killing him would be a major step in escalation for any foreign power or criminals.

The secret service game really did rely on sticking to basic rules. In essence you did not bump off each others top personell. It would make the whole situation impossible with an endless round of tit for tat killings. In any event, often security interests coincided. So your enemy on Monday may be you friend in counter terrorist activity by the end of the week, so you needed a working relationship with your counterpart and bumping them off would not be helpful in establishing one.

Stiles was in essence setting himself up as a guarantor of Jackie's and his safety. It was a gamble but he was sticking his neck out betting that no one wanted the fallout that would follow from an attack on the senior figure in a Country's Security Service.

Tim must have dozed off and woke with a start when the door bell rang. It was dark and he fumbled around eventually finding a light switch. His eyes adjusted and he looked at his watch it was one thirty in the morning.

He opened the door. "Time to go" said Stiles.

Chapter 33

It had been a long twenty four hours for Trist and Annubis. Unable to just drive into the Rojas hacienda they had to trek to the kill position. Undercover of darkness they made the eighteen or so mile journey. The night air proved to be chillier than they had anticipated and the lack of a moon had made the journey very uncomfortable.

Enrique Rojas was not a stupid man and made sure regular patrols protected his property and there were surveillance cameras that served the dual purpose of checking the animals and checking for intruders. They were equipped with night glasses which at least gave them the opportunity to check their route and avoid the cameras that were mounted high up on long metal poles.

The route they had chosen was the shortest from the road. Their goal was a building under construction that was destined to be some sort of exotic animal compound in the future. At this stage, however, it was just a shell surrounded by scaffolding with a large flat roof. They had selected that precise location as it both offered a view of the main house and its grounds with garden and swimming pool and it also offered the flat roof upon which the helicopter would be able to extract them after the kills.

They had driven to their start point and abandoned the car. It had been pushed into a deep gully that ran alongside of the road. They had taken considerable care to cut brush, scrub and foliage to completely conceal the vehicle. Satisfied that it could not be seen from the road or air they had gathered their gear, including the two sniper rifles and headed into the darkness.

They maintained silence as they progressed to their hideout. Trist wished that he could just have taken the opportunity under the cover of darkness to shoot Annubis in the back. That would have been so less risky and simple. Rojas on the other hand had stipulated that he wanted him alive. He also wanted Rodriguez out of the way. The death of Rodriguez at the hands of Annubis was ideal. Rojas got his Father's killer, the death of a rival and the bonus of shifting the guilt for the assignation of Rodriguez onto the Americans.

Trist soon realised that his companion was in a different league to himself when it came to mental and physical toughness. Annubis just kept going and soon Trist found it hard to maintain the pace being set. When he called for a rest his companion just seemed to be bemused by the need to halt. Annubis said nothing and just waited silently while Trist caught his breath.

After five hours of walking they were coming upon the animal compounds. Their progress had been considerably slower than they had anticipated, due in the main to Trist. The wire fence was stretched before them and dawn was rapidly approaching. Their planned route called for a sizeable detour to avoid contact with the inhabitants of the fenced in enclosure.

Annubis stopped, "We do not have the time to go round."

"Do you know what is behind that fence?" said Trist.

"It is of no consequence. If we are not in position by the time the Sun rises we will be seen and killed." He took some metal cutters from his pack and began to cut a hole in the ten foot high, chain link fence.

"Are you fucking mad, there are lions in there?"

Annubis looked at Trist and at that point Trist realised this man was fearful of nothing. The lack of fear was borne from the fact, he realised, that this Annubis wanted death. In fact he longed for it. In that instant Trist realised that he was looking into the eyes of the most dangerous of all creatures, a man who had had enough of life and placed no value on it. His was, in his heart, already no longer of the living but in the company of the departed.

Trist said nothing, further realising that his chances of survival were greater facing lions than they were facing this man.

They were soon the wrong side of the fence. Annubis had made a very big hole in the fence as he saw little disadvantage in having a pride of lions joining Rojas's planned get together with the other drug barons later that day. In fact they could prove a worth while distraction.

Annubis picked up the pace and headed straight across the lion enclosure, Trist was forcing himself to keep going. The fear was almost crippling him and his legs felt like they were as heavy as lead. His companion on the other hand seemed oblivious to the threat and walked confidently ahead. Their journey continued and their short cut seemed to have paid off as the ring fence came into view ahead. Trist actually did breathe a sigh of relief as they were within a few hundred feet of getting out of the lion enclosure. He exhaled loudly.

"Shut the fuck up," said Annubis. "A lion has been stalking us for the last ten minutes. Stand still and don't move."

Trist became aware of the movement in the bushes to their left. His whole body screamed at him to run and he began to shake. He could smell the lion as the beast was up wind of them and he could hear a feint but distinct growling. Annubis had turned towards the lion which had its tail stiff and twitched it. It was in hunting mode and he and Annubis were its intended prey.

Any second the lion would pounce. They could attempt to shoot it with their side arms but that, as far as Annubis was concerned, was just a different way to sign their own death warrants as the sound of gunshot would bring the guards to them. Trist decided he would use his gun on the lion and hope that in the inevitable confrontation that would follow with Rojas's men he wouldn't end up dead.

Without warning Annubis let out an almighty ear shattering scream and turned on his powerful flashlight shinning it directly into the Lion's eyes. The suddenness of it and the brightness of the beam caused the lion to stop in its tracks, turn tail and run off into the darkness Annubis just carried on walking to the fence and removed the chain cutters from his pack. Trist on the other hand found that his legs had turned to jelly as he stumbled to catch up. One thing he was sure of was that taking this man alive had handing him to Rojas may prove a lot more difficult that he had imagined it would be.

Annubis was also having doubts about the ability of Trist to deliver a clean hit. He had seen the weakness in the man. He now felt contempt for Trist. He had no choice but to continue however. He had never failed to complete a contract and this would not be the one he would fail on.

First light saw them in position on the roof of the partially completed building. They were nearly a mile from the compound were Rojas would later that day be hosting his little get together. Trist had gone through the motions with Annubis of sighting his rifle and placing it on the tripod for the hits to come. His target was Rojas. In truth he had no chance at all of shooting the man from this distance even with the latest rifle and technology at his finger tips. Fortunately he had no intention of trying to do so. He was fairly confident however, that Rodriguez was facing his last day on the planet with Annubis taking the shot.

"Are you sure you can rely on this helicopter pilot?" asked Annubis.

"Yes, the CIA have used him many times," lied Trist.

Chapter 34

Tim and Stiles were feeling the tension as they drove along the coast road. It was two in the morning and the Moon sat low on the horizon over the Libyan Sea. The Moon was far larger than Tim was used to in Northern Europe and it was unsettling as it seemed to dominate the seascape. The sky was cloudless and it made the presence of the Moon all that more imposing. It felt like it was actually watching them and they felt exposed and on view to all.

They found the track that led into the hills and started the bumpy ride upwards. They eventually arrived at the sleeping Greek village with its narrow streets and passed through it onwards and up the mountain. The road turned into a track and the olive trees gave way to scrub and rocky outcrops of limestone covered in sparse clumps of grass that had turned brown in the daily Sunshine.

The track eventually ran out. There was no agriculture beyond this point, even the hardy Cretan goats would struggle to find sufficient sustenance to survive on the plateau. They bumped along the rocky ground continuing their journey to the grid reference they had been given by Jackie's captures.

Stiles stopped the vehicle as they saw a parked jeep with its headlights on in front of them. Their eyes accustomed themselves to the new source of light and they could see two men standing either side of the waiting jeep. It was clear that they were armed with some type of semi automatic weapon, the details of which could not be discerned from where they had stopped.

They looked at each other to gain courage and support and taking deep breaths they opened the doors and stepped out into the beam of their own headlights. They advanced a few steps and were very conscious of the guns pointing at them. They stopped.

"Are you alone?" one of the shadowy figures called out in a thick Russian accent.

Stiles always given to facetiousness even surprised himself at the belligerence of his reply. "No we have Custer and the 7th Calvary in our pockets. Don't be fucking stupid."

The man raised a mobile phone or radio, it was hard to see with the light source from the car headlights often turning the figures into silhouettes as they passed in font of the beams, to his mouth. "Wait," he shouted back at them.

They waited. They waited for what seemed hours facing each other but it was a matter of eight or nine minutes. With the heightened sense of reality that comes with the increase in adrenaline in their veins, everything from the moment they stood in front of these men seemed to be moving in slow motion.

The sound of rotor blades could be heard first, followed by the intense beam of the searchlight. They felt the downdraft whipping up the dust, debris and small, loose stones. The helicopter had left the deck of the Lady Heloise with Yerik and Jackie on board about seven minutes earlier, having had the all clear from the man facing Tim and Stiles. It did not land immediately but scoured the plateau with its searchlight looking for any intruders to the meeting. Apparently satisfied that they were alone, the helicopter descended behind the two men and the jeep. The blades slowly came to rest and the whirl of the engine died. There was a strange calm that settled on the scene as the players were in place but not yet moving.

Tim felt his heart begin to pound as he saw his wife and Yerik step from the helicopter with a third man, Yerik's bodyguard. The pilot remained seated in the craft and the three moved into the area lit by the vehicles' headlights.

Jackie began to shout as she saw Tim. Yerik told her to be quiet and spoke himself.

"There is no need for dramatics. You have something of mine and I have something of yours, Mr Burr. We swap and we all go home to our beds."

"Release my wife first," Tim found his voice seemed to be coming from a distance, not from his mouth and his fear was betrayed in it shakiness.

"Of course but my men will shoot her if you do not produce the documents before she reaches you. Is that understood?"

Tim reached into the car and held up the envelope that Maurice had posted to Jackie. "They are all here," he shouted his voice now calmer.

Yerik gave Jackie a gentle push in Tim's direction and Yerik's bodyguard fell in behind her, pointing a pistol at her head as they walked forward. Tim set out holding the documents held clearly visible before him. Stiles moved alongside him.

The stopped facing one another. There was a tense brief moment when Tim feared that Jackie's guard would shoot her then turn his gun on Tim, but that fear was unjustified. Tim held out his hand proffering the envelope. The body guard took it. "Do not move."

Tim looked into Jackie's face. He saw the small tear in her eyes, a tear of relief and joy. He felt a wave of love and the need to protect her and went to move forward to sweep her into his arms, to hold her close and feel the warmth of her body. Stiles reached out and touched his forearm restraining from acting pre-emptively.

The bodyguard opened the envelope and using his flashlight he inspected the papers. "They are the originals," he shouted back to

Yerik.

Tim stepped forword and throwing his arms around Jackie, pulled her to him and kissed her. He turned quickly and half pushed her and half pulled her to their waiting car. He wanted her exposed for as little time as possible. Stiles was bringing up the rear.

"Kill them," shouted Yerik. He had wisely decided that it would be best to clear up all the loose ends while he had the chance. He turned towards his waiting chopper.

Tim reacted quickly and threw Jackie to the ground as a shot rang out. Stiles, being between the couple and the shooter did not fare as well. The bullet hit him in the back. He fell forward onto his face.

The bushes and rocks scattered across the plateau suddenly came to life, following the shot from the bodyguard. Almost instantly a second shot rang out and the bodyguard dropped to his knees. Red dots appeared in the middle of the foreheads of Yerik, his two gunmen and the pilot. The body guard also had the laser sight dot clearly visible reflected on his face as he groaned on the ground.

The Marines had appeared as if by magic, emerging from the landscape where they had been camouflaged and concealed in plain sight. They had been deployed hours before the meeting was due to take place. Their concealment was so professional that one of their number had only been six or seven feet from where Yerik stood and he seemed to morph from part of the landscape in to a man as if by magic.

The Marine reached forward and removed the documents from Yerik's hand. Yerik was plainly shocked by the sudden turn of events. His confusion was only heightened as the deafening roar of the Agusta Westland AW159 Wildcat helicopter hovering above them.

"Now that's what you call a helicopter," said the Marine. "Now fuck off back to your boat. Take your wounded mate with you. Do not even think of trying to do anything in your silly little chopper or our Wildcat will blast it out of existence."

Yerik, with the help from the other two now disarmed gunmen dragged the bodyguard back to the chopper. Tim watched as they all boarded the chopper which took off and flew back to the Lady Heloise.

They were trailed back by the Wildcat. When they landed on the deck of the Lady Heloise, they were surrounded by a joint boarding party from HMS Defender and the Greek Navy.

"Now old boy, you have really made a bit of a nuisance of yourself abducting EU citizens," said Captain Stanley Jones. "People smuggling is very serious and we are working with our Greek allies in a bid to protect the EU boarders." Jones knew full well that this was not a case of people trafficking but it was all the excuse needed for naval intervention.

"Now we have decided to be very generous with you and let you go. You will sail out of these waters straight back to Monaco. Please be clear that when I say straight back, I do mean straight back. No passing "go", no stopping, no flying your little helicopter and no launching your tender. All of you get out the area. I hope you fully understand me. We will be tracking you and please be aware we can spot a fly landing on your nose from twenty miles, so don't try and mess with us. You should also be aware that we have orders that allow us to blow the suspected people traffickers out of the water if they do not comply with our instructions. You, my friend, have been classified officially in the people smuggler category. Get the picture, in other words piss off."

"Yes I have the picture," said Yerik.

"Fucking hell that hurt," said Stiles as Tim helped him to his feet.

"These vest may be heavy but they obviously work," said Tim.

BANK

Holding Jackie's hand with one hand and holding the envelope in the other he sat in the back of the jeep as Stiles drove them back down the mountain to their hotel.

Chapter 35

It was nearly four in the morning when the three of them arrived back at the Golf Resort Hotel. The sky was turning a yellowy orange as the Sun made its way above the horizon. Tim and Stiles were on the terrace looking at the Sunrise. Jackie was on the phone in the bedroom talking to an elated Daniel.

"That was more exciting than you would have thought. You could have told me about the special forces?" said Tim.

"There seemed little point. I figured that they would not shoot us until they were sure we had the evidence with us. Then I was sort of hoping that they would stick to the bargain and just swap Jackie and go. If they didn't it was always going to be a free for all, so I just made sure we had the odds stacked in our favour."

Jackie could be heard in the other room saying her goodbyes. "I shall be getting off to bed now," said Stiles and picked up the envelope.

"I think you should leave that and let Jackie deal with it. After all is said and done, her friend died for it and she has been through hell for it. She should have the satisfaction of exposing the bastards," said Tim.

Stiles replaced the envelope on the dining table and calling out his good nights to Jackie left.

Jackie walked from the bedroom naked. "I thought I should take a shower."

Tim just stood and stared. He felt his emotions begin to well up inside of him. She was alive and so beautiful. She saw how affectionately he was looking at her and twilled around slowly allowing him to appreciate he body. He stepped forward and held her close. She felt the tension ebb from his body as he took her in his arms and kissed long and gently on her lips. She felt the tension return to him in the form of his arousal pressing into her stomach.

"I am guessing you prefer your women dirty then. I'll skip the shower then, shall I?" she stepped back in the bedroom and lay on her back on the bed. "Fuck me Mr Burr," she said.

The love making was intense. They both felt deep inside that this opportunity to be intimate could so easily have been taken away from them forever had things gone badly on the mountain earlier. They felt the urgency, almost like two virgins experimenting for the first time, a mixture of feral lust and wonderment that they were making love.

They fucked hard and long until they felt they could fuck no more. Tired and lying in a crumpled bed, they fell into a contented sleep clinging tightly to each other. Happy and relieved that they lived and still loved.

They were awakened by the sound of an embarrassed maid, whom they had not heard knock and had entered their bedroom wheeling a cart with new bed linen on it. They giggled as she retreated from their apartment

It was late," We have missed breakfast," said Tim as he made his way to the bathroom to perform his morning ablutions. He emerged shaved and showered. He dressed as Jackie climbed out of the somewhat dishevelled bed. "You get dressed and I shall make us brunch."

"There's no food."

"Small point, I'll wake Stiles. Get the car keys off him and go to the shops. Then the three of us can eat on the terrace here."

She was in the shower when he left. He made his way, followed by a stray cat which seemed to wait at the door of the apartment for his emergence, to Stiles' room. He knocked several times before, a bleary eyed, Stiles opened the door.

"What time is it?"

"Late, we have missed breakfast. Jackie is getting dressed and I thought I would drive down the hill and forage for food. Get yourself dressed and then go to Jackie's and my apartment where I shall return with brunch and serve it on the terrace. Give me the car keys."

Driving down the road from the resort to the coast, Tim could not have felt happier. The sea and sky were a deep azure blue. There was a gentle breeze that wafted the scent of gardenia and pine into the morning air. He had a beautiful wife. He had never felt so content and happy. He even turned on the radio and was in such a happy place that he actually tapped along to the rhythm of the bouzouki ensemble coming from the speakers.

Chapter 39

The meeting was becoming extremely heated. Rojas sat at the head of the long dining table in the opulent dining room, in his over decorated villa. It was mid afternoon and the group of eight drug cartel members had finished lunch. The drink and drugs were beginning to take their effect on the participants and rationality was giving way to anger.

"Why, the fuck have you not been hit? All the rest of us have lost millions in the drug seizures over the past few months and you, you my friend seemed to be immune from the DEA?"

"What is that supposed to mean? Are you accusing me of being a rat?" Rodriguez was incandescent with rage and small globs of spittle leapt from his mouth as he ranted.

Rojas was silently pleased with the groundswell of resentment among his colleagues which was building against Rodriguez. This anger would make it all the easier for him to have him killed and for the other members not to baulk against his actions. Greed was a wonderful thing and they would all benefit from having a key player removed and he would benefit the most.

"Gentlemen, gentlemen let's not let this descend into a free for all. We have no proof against anyone at the table and we need to keep this under control. We do not need this disagreement to descend into another war between us, if that happens we all lose and the authorities will have international pressure put on them to act. We need to resolve this in a business like fashion,"said Rojas.

"That is easy for you to say. You are the richest and most

powerful," interrupted a disgruntled voice.

"May I remind you I have also had the largest seizure, the first and most costly?"

There was a murmur of agreement around the table and Rojas was satisfied to know that he had established himself as a victim and not the perpetrator. "We are listening" said one of their number."

"Insurance," said Rojas

"What the fuck you say?"

"Insurance," repeated Rojas. "We do what legitimate business does, we insure ourselves against the loss of our goods."

"Who insures drug shipments, American Life?" there was laughter around the table.

"We do. We spread the risk among ourselves. When one of us loses the rest of us chip in a share of the loss."

There was a rare moment of silence as the assembled chewed over the idea. Rojas, of course, would be the net beneficiary of any such arrangement by making sure the information he fed to the DEA would ensure that he had sufficient losses to avoid suspicion, whilst recouping most of the lost revenue from his fellow drug barons. "It has the added benefit that anyone who rats also ends up paying for the loss incurred. A big disincentive I would argue," he continued to push the point.

"Enough for today, let's get to the party." He led the way to the swimming pool area. He would let the idea rest with them for the present.

Annubis and Trist were feeling the effects of the heat as they waited on the roof of the half finished building. They had a long wait. They had seen the limousines pull up with the drug lords and their bodyguards and watched as they headed into Rojas' villa. Then they just sat and waited. They had a perfect view of the pool complex.

Not until mid afternoon did activity commence in the outside area. Food and drink was laid out. Sun umbrellas opened and about twenty totally naked girls appeared and scattered themselves decoratively around the patio. Rojas certainly knew how to throw a party and please his guests. The mariachi band began to play as the guests emerged into the Sunlight. The naked girls flocked to the men and encouraged them to start shedding their clothing.

Annubis and Trist settled into their firing positions. They looked through scope sights on the sniper rifles and began to seek out their respective targets. Rojas was an easy target standing to one side and watching the building orgy. Rodriguez was proving a harder target for Annubis as he was surrounded by three young women who kept coming between him and the clean headshot he wanted.

Trist announced that he had acquired his target and was ready to take the shot. Annubis waited patiently controlling his breathing. His time would come and he knew patience was everything and he had learned to have plenty of it.

Finally "I have shot," declared Annubis

"Fire," said Trist.

Annubis slowly squeezed the trigger and a brief instant later the full metal jacket bullet exploded in Rodriguez's head and sprayed blood and brains all over the naked blonde girl who was sucking on his penis.

Annubis looked at Rojas and was staggered to see that he was unarmed. He then felt the barrel of Trist's rifle pressed against the base of his skull. "Don't move." Trist kicked the Annubis's rifle out of his reach and stood in silence with his gun pointing at him as he lay face down on the roof.

There was confusion at the party and the all the drug lords ran for cover into the villa. Rojas could not help feeling slightly amused as he watched a load of, in the main flabby arsed, middle aged men running with the trousers round their ankles. Rojas's men jumped into a couple of jeeps and headed to the building where Trist awaited their arrival. They would bring Annubis to Rojas where he would be exposed as a CIA assassin. Trist would be given a lift to his vehicle and get his payoff. Rojas had his revenge for his Father's murder and he had the added bonus of getting rid of Rodriquez.

Chapter 37

Tim remembered seeing the petrol station and the Lidl opposite when Stiles and he had been heading for their rendezvous the previous evening. He slowed the jeep down and waited at the lights for an opportunity to turn left into the supermarket. They changed to green and he entered the car park and parked in a space under one of the Sun awnings that provided shade for the vehicles.

He realised he did not have the requisite Euro to release the shopping cart, but found the baskets as he entered the doors to the shop. To his surprise they stocked all the ingredients for the good old British fry up. Having grabbed the eggs, bacon and some Greek sausages, he decided that he ought to consider a healthier option as an alternative. The healthier option consisted of some croissants, jam and orange juice. Satisfied with his selection Tim headed for the check out.

Passing up the aisles he came across the bargain of the month section. All types of odd items were piled in baskets at what were at, apparently, very low prices. Tim was drawn to the random collection of items for sale. There were drills, zillion watt flashlights and even some crampons. Tim decided they would probably not be doing any mountaineering that day but was drawn to the toys. He thought of Daniel. They had bought souvenirs in Egypt but they had all been lost in their sudden and unforeseen mode of departure.

"Super Extreme Soaker," proclaimed the packaging, "fires a high pressure jet of water up to twenty metres." Tim had to have two. He pictured Daniel and him spraying and chasing each other in the back garden, before turning their soakers on an unsuspecting

Jackie. He would be glad to get all of them home safe and back as a family again.

Carrying the carrier bag and the two large boxed super extreme soakers back to the Jeep proved somewhat more challenging than he envisaged. After dropping a few things, fortunately not the eggs, he managed to dump the fruits of his expedition into the rear of the vehicle. He started the engine and turned right onto the main road. The lights turned green at the junction and he crossed to the far lane and began accelerating up the hill.

As he approached the crest, a bus came hurtling towards him on his side of the road. His brain froze as the bus raced towards him, lights flashing and horn blaring. Finally, he reacted and pulled the jeep from the road. He bounced across the gravel that bordered the highway and after a bumpy ride came to rest in a grove of olive trees. His heart was racing and he sat stunned breathing heavily. He had stopped inches from an old gnarly tree. A few feet further and a little more speed and he would have been another casualty on the notorious Greek roads.

"How could I be so fucking stupid," he said aloud to himself. Having calmed down he realised while daydreaming about returning home to Daniel he had let his concentration slip. The layout of the junction had not helped but it was his own fault that he had driven on the left. Stupid, stupid, how could he be so stupid? After all they had been through he had nearly killed himself by driving on the British side of the road, left, while most of the rest of the World drove on the right.

He composed himself and his drive back to the Golf resort was far more sedate then it had been on his leaving. He found a place in the main car park and began his walk back towards their apartment. He left the soakers and decided they could be parked in the diplomatic box with the other weaponry. He was soon joined by the inevitable cat, who was also interested in what there was for breakfast in the plastic bag.

BANK

He managed to open the door and enter the apartment without the cat joining him inside. He looked through, past the dining area, past the seating area and could see through the open terrace doors and flapping curtains a glimpse of Stiles' arm resting on a chair arm as he sat on the patio. Jackie and he were relaxing and enjoying the Sun and the spectacular views to the mountains across the rear garden area.

"Stay where you are. I shall make you both a gourmet fry up and bring it out to you." He turned to his left and entered the kitchen area. After pulling out every draw and opening every cupboard, he eventually assembled the necessary pans, crockery and cutlery to complete the process. Randomly pressing buttons on the hob he managed to get the hot plates to do what they were designed to do, get hot.

"Can you stop the cats getting in," he shouted after he drove another stray out of the kitchen.

He received no response and feeling slightly irritated he made his way out of the kitchen to ask them to pull the french doors to a bit, in order to cut the feline incursions into the apartment. He noticed that the envelope that he had left on the dining table the previous night had been removed. He called again to Stiles and Jackie who he could see with their backs to him on the patio.

They were surround by six or seven strays licking at something that was pooling on the terrace. He walked through the lounge and past the sofa and chairs. As he came to the window he saw that the liquid was red and viscous.

"No," he screamed. It was a whale of agony, tortured pain, a cry of total despair.

They liquid being gratefully lapped up by the cats was blood, the blood of his wife and his best friend. They were slumped back in the chairs. Both had been shot neatly in the middle of the forehead.

Both had died instantly. Their killer had then climbed over the low trellis surrounding the terrace, walked in and left with the envelope that had been on the dining table.

He slumped to his knees, tears rolling down his cheeks and gradually curled up into a ball.

Chapter 38

Annubis knew that this was the end. He knew that it was always bound to come to a conclusion in this manner. He had judged men and killed men. He had spent his life seeking revenge for the death of his family and his brother. His own soul had been forfeit many years ago when he had committed the murder of the pig in charge of the Children's home in Turkey, where he and his brother had suffered so much. He had gloried in revenge and the blood of those who had killed his Father in Iraq. He had released all his anger on the murderers of his innocent younger brother, torturing them and hacking them to pieces.

Now, as he stood wracked in pain before his tormentor Rojas, he realised he had been destined from the inception to deal in death. Fate had laid the path out ahead and he had embraced it, followed it without even considering deviating from his calling.

He knew he had no need to be in this position. He had more wealth than he could ever spend. The murder of Rojas for money was what he did and he had no way of stopping. No brake he could apply. He had no other purpose but to continue killing and profiting by the bodies he piled up. Now, at the end, he wondered if he should fear remorse or regret. He felt what he had always felt, isolation and hatred.

Rojas had him beaten. The pain was there but it made him feel elated, almost in a state of euphoria as they punched, kicked, cut, slashed and used clubs to break bone and mangle flesh. He had risen to a higher state, absorbing the pain and entering a half dead state where clarity came to him. It was his punishment and his cleansing. He needed this punishment and the destruction of his body.

The picture of his brother being taken from the orphanage that night played in his head on a continuous loop, Mehmet and the car, his brother being led by the hand, the car leaving. Through the pain and the blood he saw it again and again.

It was he. He had stood and watched and done nothing as the little, trusting boy with big olive shaped eyes, skipped, excited, holding the hand of his abuser. Innocent and unaware of what was to happen to him, unknowing. Happy to hold the hand of the man that would have him used, to satisfy the perverted sexual cravings of the privileged men that waited to use him for an evening's entertainment. A small boy excited at having a ride in a shiny car. A boy whose parents had been murdered, a boy with nothing left but his tiny small, gentle life.

He did nothing, He did not warn him. He just watched. But worse, far worse, he had been the ultimate betrayer. He had saved himself. He had supposed to go that night. He had been before to the parties. He had felt the pain, the humiliation and he knew what awaited him. He had heard the orphanage pig of a manager talking on the phone and knew they were coming to collect boys for their party.

He had abandoned his brother and climbed out of the building and hid. That left the manager short on his delivery of young boys. His brother was too small to take the abuse, but the pig in charge wanted his money and sent him anyway.

He had felt relief as he hid. Relief of all things as the tiny boy was taken to be abused and killed. He had sacrificed his brother. His hatred of himself had always far outweighed the hatred he held for the scum that had actually killed his brother.

Now stood there in Mexico, a shredded, bloody, half conscious, and twisted dying man he at last felt peace. He had deserved this punishment. He had craved this all his life. He felt cleansed and reborn.

"I have the confession from the bastard who murdered our colleague," Rojas was addressing the drug lords on the terrace. In one fell swoop he had enjoyed the taste of vengeance as he tortured his Father's killer and had his biggest rival killed. "Rodriguez was the rat and the CIA sent this man to kill him to cover it up."

"Why would they kill their own informant?"

"He was becoming an embarrassment to them. He was threatening them with exposure to Congress. He wanted more than power and money here. He wanted immunity from prosecution in the US. He was just too greedy." Rojas knew that the link was tenuous but it fitted the facts and the other Cartel members were too weak to challenge him in any event.

"Come let's visit the animals." They made their way to the waiting offroaders. Rojas had the jeeps painted in black and white zebra strips. They were off on safari in the middle of Mexico. Annubis was dumped on a flat bed and the party set off.

The Sun was beginning to descend and the sky was turning a beautiful shade of orange. They stood at the edge of the lake, the calm reflected in the flickering orange and red of the evening sky. Annubis was dragged into the shallow bottomed boat and a life jacket put on to ensure he would float. Two of Rojas's men slowly rowed to the centre of the lake.

The body was carefully and silently lowered into the calm waters of the lake and the men hastened to the shore. Annubis could be seen floundering, moving erratically and splashing far from shore. He became still and seemed to lay twitching on the surface.

Without warning the huge mouth, wide open broke through the surface. The hippopotamus enraged by the intrusion into its territory attacked the half dying man. Almost majestically its jaws snapped shut around the body and ground down on it. The body exploded in mass of raw meat and blood. The hippo opened its mouth wide a second time before the crushing power of its jaws cut the body almost in half. It sank slowly down into the lake.

All was calm. The assembled group watched as the surface bubbled and the air trapped in the body forced bits of it to bob to the surface. They Sun set as the crushed and mangled remains of Annubis finally sank from view.

Chapter 39

Elaine, the head of MI5, sat looking out from the window. It was a very overcast day, grey with clouds that hung low casting a deep shadow across the landscape. Never had she known such bleak times. She wore a black suit and black shoes. For once her foot wear held no pleasure for her. This was the second day in a row she was dressed in black. Yesterday she had buried her deputy Jeff Stiles, today she would attend the funeral of Jacqueline Burr.

She looked over at her husband, wheelchair bound now. She remembered them as a young couple full of hope but ten years ago. The disease had taken hold and day on day his condition worsened. His full time nurse entered the room and cleaned the saliva from around his mouth and changed the wet bib that was now a constant feature of what remained of his life.

MI5 was now all to her. She felt like she was doing some good and that mostly she had a purpose. Today and yesterday she was not so sure that she did have a purpose. She took a deep breath and checked her watch. Her son would be here soon. He was always on time.

Her son, her only child would drive her to Jackie's funeral. She had done all in her power and using the CD passports, she had expedited the return of Jackie's and Stiles' bodies to the UK. It was not much but it was something.

Stile's funeral had been hard to bear. His widow and his bemused two year old daughter had just stood in shocked silence as the coffin was lowered into the ground. Tim had stood alone. He had no words of consolation for the grieving widow. He was himself so cloaked in grief that he had no sympathy to offer and was incapable of receiving any consolation either. Neither could afford the other any solace. The tragedy of it was too much for the human heart to comprehend.

Today the whole pantomime would be replayed. Nothing could be done to bring comfort to those that survived.

The doorbell rang and Elaine picked up her handbag, kissed her husband in the forehead and made her way to her son's waiting Bentley. He had put to good use the expensive private education and used his contacts and talent to become exceedingly wealthy. He was dressed in a Saville Row tailored sombre suit and wore a back tie. He looked the part of the successful millionaire businessman he was. Elaine felt a justified Motherly pride as he opened the door to the rear of the car. She sat in the back as he played chauffeur to her in the front. They pulled away and the two special branch officers, who acted as her security, followed behind in the high powered BMW.

Tim felt sick to the pit of his stomach as he sat alone in the Daimler following the hearse. Jackie's Mother, Father and Daniel were in taxi behind. Her Father was in a wheelchair and the only way to transport him had been the use of the black cab fitted with a disabled access ramp. There had been little conversation between them on his return and Daniel had refused to engage with him at all. So he sat alone on his way to bury his wife.

The progress was slow and he felt claustrophobic in the rear of the oversized car. The walls of the vehicle seemed to be pressing down on him and sucking the air from him. He knew he was in shock but that did not help in anyway to prevent his brain giving him a panic attack. He just kept replaying the same morning in Crete. Why had he gone alone to shop for breakfast? They could easily have found a place to eat breakfast. She would not have been there and the killer would merely have broken in and taken the file. They would be alive now. So many permutations kept going through his head. That one decision to leave his wife sat on the terrace had resulted in this outcome. Two people dead and two orphaned children.

They reached Finchley Crematorium and turned into the sweeping drive leading to the Chapel. The car pulled up and he sat numbed in the car. The driver had to rouse him. His legs were like lead as he stepped from the car. He was aware of the mourners, Jackie's Mother crying, her Dad crying and the small forlorn figure of Daniel grasping at his grandmother's hand desperately, as though she might also be snatched from him.

The coffin was lifted from the hearse and shouldered by the hired bearers. He followed the slow moving procession and watched, dazed as the coffin was placed on the trestle in the middle of the raised dais.

After that it all became words, a hymn, a reading. His eulogy was just words, words that conveyed nothing. He felt nothing of the woman he loved. It was futile and totally failed to give comfort. It merely increased his sense of loss and isolation.

Finally the coffin disappeared behind the curtains on the conveyor that would incinerate her body. Now only memories would remain, so few memories, but such precious ones that they would have to sustain him for a lifetime.

He walked out into the damp, grey afternoon air. The World seemed to reflect his mood and became a darker, colder lonelier place. He walked to Daniel and extended his arms to pull him close. At least one small part of her lived, a tangible part that he could still hold and comfort.

Daniel pulled back as if he had been pulled onto a hot poker. Tim saw the look of pure hatred in his eyes.

"You promised," he cried through thick tears. "She's dead, you promised. You killed my mummy. I hate you."

Tim recoiled, struck by the shear anguish and grief of this small, lonely child.

As Annubis died far away in Mexico, in a cold wet crematorium across the other side of the World, the hatred that had driven him on his path of death and suffering was reborn in Tim. Tim knew his path was set. He would find and kill everyone that had a hand in his wife's death. Annubis was reborn

Chapter 40

Graham Pelham gazed out of the window at the grey Manx sky and watched the raindrops slowly run down the glass of the office window of the law firm in Athol Street. His gaze was unfocussed as he sat deep in thought. On his desk was a packet, as yet unopened. His decision that day was if he should open the envelope?

The client to whom the packet belonged had been introduced by the dodgy, ex convict, New York banker, Mel Levy. Pelham had to concede that Levy for all his faults had made a great deal of money for him personally and his firm of advocates. The Russians and their money laundering alone had allowed him to amass a small fortune.

He was being paid twenty thousand pounds a year just to store the packet sitting on his desk. The only other duty he had to perform to earn his money was to check his email. Each month a message would appear reading "Annubis lives." As long as the message appeared on time in his in box his duty was complete.

This month, however the message had failed to arrive. He had now waited a further five days and there still had been no communication. He could wait no longer. Along with the packet entrusted to him for safe keeping had been a letter addressed to him. That letter was held in his hand as he looked out the window contemplating his next course of action.

The letter read, "Dear Mr Pelham, enclosed is a package that you should delivery personally to the addressee. Upon completion of this task the sum of one million pounds will be transferred to you designated bank account."

Pelham swivelled his chair round and placed the parcel on his desk. He picked it up and read the name on the front. Mr Anthony Burr, Thames House London.

He knew that the Headquarters of MI5 was based in Thames House. It was indeed a dilemma. He wanted a million pounds, but he did not want to bring himself to the attention of one of the Worlds most successful anti terrorist organisations, particularly as he was up to his neck in helping some of the richest Russians clean their ill gotten gains.

He sat a while longer. The draw of an extra million pounds got the better of him and his greed won the argument. He rationalised that he would meet with this Mr Burr at MI5 and feel out the ground. He would skirt the issue and then decide if he should hand him the packet or not. He would come up with a cover story about clarifying some legal technicality and take it from there.

He picked up the phone to his secretary. "Could you get me MI5, they are based in Thames House in London," he said.

The phone call took considerably longer than he had imagined. Had he thought about it he would have realised that MI5 was subjected to thousands of crank calls a year. It would be necessary to apply some form of filter system, or all their resources would be tied up dealing with calls from people. For example who had met an alien in the park the previous evening.

Tim was sat at his desk and not engaging in the World around him. His first reaction had been to resign. In truth he no longer had any interest in scrutinising the minutia of the thousands of often unconnected bits of information that appeared on his desk. GCHQ spent hours up on hours sifting, sorting and collating source information and then it was analysed initially by a computer seeking connections and cross referencing to all the databases available to MI5 before, finally, it was subjected to human touch. A file, usually electronic, was passed to him as head of section for the final judgement call. Resources were scarce and so precious. Following up on one situation meant that the opportunity to investigate another had to be forgone.

At one time he had revelled in making these judgement calls and gained immense satisfaction in finding, more often than not, he had made the correct choice. Now with the murder of his wife, he was in truth embittered and no longer cared. He felt resentment against the World that had taken her away from him.

He had not resigned and was now using the resources of the Agency to further his own agenda of identifying the actual killer of his wife and colleague. His file on the Russians was growing by the day. Their connections to others were being traced. Covertly he was building a dossier as detailed as any on these people and their associates. Somewhere there would be a link, a tiny scrap, a morsel of information that would lead him to the person or persons that had walked up to that terrace and without a second thought had put a bullet in her head.

Yerik and his bunch of thugs were on the Lady Heloise watched by a great big battleship. Nikhil and Lesta were in another part of the planet miles away. They could all be ruled out as the actual killer who had pulled the trigger. They were as guilty, of course and they would pay but not before he had his man. It was a matter of time but he would find him. And in the end he would have his vengeance.

The phone rang and he was minded to ignore it. He felt though, perhaps he ought to engage at least a little in genuine MI5 business and decided to answer it. It was one of the junior staff members. She had only worked at MI5 a few months and had been recruited straight from University. A more experienced team member would probably discount the call and not bothered the head of section. In her keenness to not make mistakes early in her career, she had opted for the better safe than sorry course of action and picked up the phone to her boss.

"A lawyer from the Isle of Man wants to speak to you," she said.

"Just take his details and make a note of what he says and pass it into the pool for analysis."

"No he wants to talk to you specifically. He asked for you by name, he said it was very important."

Tim was not inclined to indulge this lawyer. However the fact he was a lawyer did promote him above the usual unsolicited phone callers.

"Put him through."

"This is Tim Burr please be brief."

"My name is Graham Pelham, I am a Manx advocate and I am contacting you on behalf of a client."

"Perhaps it would be better if your client contacted us direct. Information provided anonymously is hard to evaluate you understand. Please ask your client to contact the relevant section. The phone in service provides a number of options to select from," Tim was about to hang up.

"Please wait one moment. I am to mention the name Annubis."

Tim was silent for a moment as he gathered his thoughts. "I am listening."

"I have a package that he insists that I should hand to you personally."

Chapter 41

The death of Stiles had caused somewhat of a crisis. Elaine found herself sat in the Cabinet Room in number ten Downing Street with the Prime Minister, the Foreign Secretary, the Home Secretary and representatives of the armed services, police and special branch. Elaine and the PM were the only women among the other twenty or so individuals in the room.

"Sadly the file containing the documentation linking some of the richest men in Russia and even the Kremlin to the stash of offshore money has been lost. It was I fear, an opportunity lost in terms off putting pressure on the Russians to moderate foreign policy, for example in the Middle East and even the Ukraine. The Americans are eager to hit them in the pockets where it actually matters to them. Applying sanctions has had a profound effect on the Russian economy but the wealthy are, of course, isolated from the consequences of the downturn. Seizing or freezing their bank accounts would have had the benefit of focussing their minds," Elaine rounded off her speech and sat down.

"Pity, it would have been nice to stick one on them," said Mailer, the Foreign Secretary. Elaine could only shrug her shoulders.

"How are you coping now, dear," asked the head of MI6, Elaine knew that he had no concern for her but was just highlighting the weakness in his counterpart. The fact that Tim had coerced Mailer into supporting the operation in Crete still rankled and he was not going to pass up an opportunity to point out any weakness in Elaine or MI5.

The obvious sexism in addressing her as "dear" would have to be passed over for the present. Elaine chose not to acknowledge the obvious condescension in the remark and was determined to answer factually without any sign of irritation.

The PM however intervened. "Lets' not waste time on asking each other how we are and get to the matter in hand. The untimely death of Elaine's number two does leave us with a clear problem as to who to put in his place."

"I have prepared a possible list of candidates and I am sure there will be other suggestions," Elaine's list was already in front of the people sat around the table.

There was no obvious replacement and the discussion lasted longer than the PM would have wished, but the succession at MI5 had seemed to have been settled. Before Stile's murder it had been tacitly accepted that Stile's would have succeeded her. Elaine was due for retirement in less than two years and he would have a number of years as head to test and groom a successor. In the time honoured fashion of the Civil Service, the right sort of chap would have naturally risen to heir apparent. Now a candidate needed to be plucked from the ranks to plug the gap.

It was not that there were not a number of capable candidates that had the ability. It was more the fact that most, if not all, were either the wrong side of the political spectrum, caused offence to someone or were just plain not the right sort. It came down in the end to picking someone who had done the least, rather than someone that had done too much and could prove problematical to the ambitions of others.

In the end Elaine's entire shortlist had been rejected. The PM was becoming irritated at the wrangling and infighting. It was clear that with an aging head, in the Form of Elaine, they all wanted a weak potential successor so they could further their own prominence. "Enough, I am head of the service in the final analysis and a decision needs to be made now. You can't or won't come up with a recommendation so I shall impose one," She named Elaine's new deputy.

Chapter 42

Tim has never been to the Isle of Man before and learned on his taxi ride from Ronaldsway Airport to Pelham's Office in Athol Street that Manx cats had no tails, there were no trees and he should make a wish as they drove over the Fairy Bridge. He had no idea why Annubis should make contact with him but he did know that the assassin had tried to help him to get his wife back. He was confident that Annubis wished him no ill and considered him a friend.

He paid the taxi and entered the Advocate's office, passing the walls covered with brass plaques bearing all the names of companies registered in the Isle of Man. Tim did wonder why the UK tax authorities had so much trouble with tracking down tax avoiders and evaders. He felt that a return ticket to the Isle of Man should not be beyond the budget of Her Majesty's Tax and Customs and Excise to send a chap over and make a list from the plaques in the advocate's offices in Athol Street.

He was shown straight into Pelham's office where his hand was shaken and he was asked to sit. On the desk between them were a laptop and a small brown wrapped parcel.

"This is difficult for me," began Pelham, "I was reluctant to contact you given your position. Our clients are keen to not draw attention to themselves and I am equally keen to not draw the attention of MI5 to me."

"I am not the tax man, but I will have no hesitation in examining every detail of your life if I ever get a whiff of a threat to National Security, be clear, and be very clear that you really need to stay on the right side of me and MI5."

Pelham took a deep breath and his discomfort was apparent as he continued. "Among my clients there is this man known only to me as Annubis. Each month He sends me an email and as long as those emails continue, my instructions are to do nothing. When they stop however, I was to open a sealed envelope which contained instructions for me to act on."

"Essentially you are happy to breach the "Know Your Client" legislation and act anyway without informing the Authorities?"

"Of course not, I have a certified copy of Mr Jon Jameson's passport who calls himself Annubis," He passed the photocopy of the passport across the desk.

Tim looked down at the face of a complete random stranger, certainly not the man he knew as Annubis, certified as genuine by a Panamanian firm of lawyers know to be complacent in money laundering and aiding clients in establishing fake or proxy personas.

Tim could not be bothered to comment and allowed Pelham to continue unchallenged. He did make a mental note that the man sat before him could prove highly useful at some stage to obtain information on the dodgy movers in the World. No harm he thought in MI5 and him personally, having dirt on the rich and powerful, the great and the good. These were the people that did business regularly with the Russian scum, who had been responsible for his wife and his best friend's death.

Pelham passed the package across the desk. Tim lent forward and began to unwrap it. It was clear that Pelham had had a look to see if there was any pecuniary advantage, having seen no way of lining his pocket without Tim he had no option but to carry out Annubis's instructions.

The letter read, "Dear Friend, if you are reading this I am no longer alive. The book was given to me as a child by my Father, it is all that I have of my life in Iraq before my parents died. It shows the ancient Egyptian Gods. I liked the pictures of Annubis weighing the souls of the dead against the weight of a feather. Those that are too heavy to enter the kingdom of the dead are gobbled up by Sobek, the crocodile,"

Tim looked at the tattered book written in Arabic. He understood and the image resonated with him. He felt the truth and that need for vengeance that had fuelled Annubis. He knew that fate had passed that lust to him and that he too would need to mercilessly act to cleanse the World of those who had destroyed his family.

It continued," I enclose details of an account I hold with Levy and Associates. They will have turned all my investments into cash. Simply enter the codes and the password and you are free to transfer the money into an account of your choosing. I have taken the liberty of establishing an account for you which is offshore and untraceable if you prefer to use it."

Tim looked at the attached piece of paper containing instructions to log on and access the money. He guessed that Pelham may well have already tried to do this himself but without the password would have failed. That explained why he had been forced to make contact.

"Mr Pelham will automatically receive a transfer when you first access the account of one million dollars for his discretion and services. The only thing to say is to wish you well my only friend. The password is all lower case, the name of murderer of my brother. Good luck and I hope your life fairs better than mine"

Pelham turned the laptop round to give Tim access and he began typing. Finally he was prompted for the password. He typed, "jasondelonge,"

Tim left the Isle of Man twelve million dollars richer.

BANK

Graham Pelham opened the metal box, Annubis's box. Inside were what appeared to be a diary and assorted papers. Written in Arabic he could not decipher it. He put it in his safe. He would get it translated sometime.

Chapter 43

Nobody was more surprised than Tim when he was appointed deputy head of MI5. He had the job by default. The discussions had led to an impasse on the suitability of any particular candidate. In essence he got the job because he had no time to piss anybody off, with the exception of the Foreign Secretary, Mailer. He, however, had no desire to stick a spanner in Tim's works, not while the file of his activities at the children's home was still in Tim's possession.

David Trist retired from the DEA after his failure to ensure the death of Rojas and went to Thailand with his payoff from the Drug Lord. He married a Thai woman in her late teens and bought a house where her family soon moved into with them. His body was found nine months after he was married. Throat cut in his car. His wife and her male cousin who lived in the same house as Trist were the prime suspects. During the investigation the police did uncover the fact that the cousin was in fact Trist's wife's long time lover, but that was still insufficient to gain a conviction for Trist's murder. His wife and her new husband inherited all his assets under Thai law.

Tim tried to establish contact with Daniel but the boy would never forgive him for his Mother's death. Tim did the best he could, using five million pounds of his new found wealth to establish an education and maintenance trust for him. Daniel's Grandfather died within eight months of Jackie's death through grief. His Grandmother struggled on until Daniel was seventeen and used the money Tim provided to try and get Daniel the best boarding school education she could. She passed away just before his eighteenth birthday.

BANK

Daniel had been a troubled child and he become more and more anti social in his teens. On his eighteenth birthday he came into the trust fund in his own right. He quit school the day after his birthday and went on a self indulgent spending spree. He died at the age of twenty one of an overdose in a grubby crack den in Miami.

Printed in Great Britain
by Amazon